BEYOND THE
PASSAGE OF TIME

Beyond the Passage of Time

Sukanya Sengupta

PARTRIDGE

ISBN: Softcover   978-1-4828-7295-8
             eBook   978-1-4828-7294-1

Print information available on the last page.

To order additional copies of this book, contact
Partridge India
000 800 10062 62
orders.india@partridgepublishing.com

www.partridgepublishing.com/india

For,

My ***Parents***, for giving me my roots and instilling
the values in me that made me what I am today.

My ***Husband***, for giving me the strength in my
wings to fly beyond where I believed I could.

PROLOGUE

"I swear upon my son, I will avenge the harm brought upon him; may be not immediately, but definitely." Lalu seethed in vengeance.

He kept on performing his duties religiously but kept his ears and eyes open. He stealthily sneaked past him without arousing any suspicion. The man behind the desk was busy on his mobile phone giving instructions to someone involved in his business. He coughed intermittently. Possibly a bad smoker's cough. He smoked frequently and continuously. He was oblivious to what Lalu was upto. Lalu was his trusted man.

Lalu, aka Lalchand Hirani, was a smart village chap, who had run away from his village at the tender age of 21. His father was a feudal landlord and used to employ poor farmers on his field in return of atrociously low daily wages. Lalu detested that terribly. He in no way would be a part of that. To eschew his father's business, he took the risk of running away to the nearby city of Bombay, with a meagre hundred rupees note in his pocket but a heart full of hope to establish himself there of his own calibre. With his unceasingly diligent pursuit of a job, he finally found himself at the local private nursing home, the job of a ward boy with his Bachelor of Arts degree as his only ammunition.

Lalu was happy. By the end of the month, he had earned with his sheer hard work, hundred notes of Rupees ten denomination. His first ever salary. He gradually bought a small tenement by saving small sums of money every month. He wanted a settled life. He wanted a life partner who would appreciate his steadfastness towards being a self made man rather than nagging him for earning lesser than what was expected out of a graduate. He found that quality in his then neighbour, who won over him through her sheer appreciation of Lalu's values. He also fell for her grace and benevolence. All put together, he thought, she was the only one who befitted his choice due to her innocent and truthful demeanour. They were happy with each other and his happiness doubled when within a year, Lalu fathered a handsome little child and his world was complete. His son, his Chhotu, was his world. He could do anything for him; go to any extent for him. He told his wife, "I never received love from anyone I know. Even my own father tried to use me. Only you have given me unconditional love and now you have given me the best gift I could ever imagine. I promise you today, I will bet even my life to take care of Chhotu. I will let no harm come upon him as long as I am alive."

Lalu kept on arranging the files while keeping a track of the conversation. He could only see the back of the man. The file cabinet was right at his back mounted on the wall. A huge mahogany desk lay infront of him, which was cluttered with files. Amidst artificial bones, stethoscopes, Blood Pressure monitoring machines and files, lay a small photo frame holding a photograph of a lady who looked similar to the man behind the desk. It was the same toothy smile, similar thick mop of curly hair though his was slightly receding, the same wheatish complexion, the same light eyes; even the texture of the skin looked similar. It seemed the man sitting there was the same woman in the photograph. The only difference being the small black mole on the right side of the man's chin, which was missing in the photograph.

He leaned back while speaking on the phone with his legs stretched ahead. He wore a suit which was the same blue shade as the haze of a tobacco smoke, a golden coloured tie and a white shirt. He wore an expensive red tape shoe and an equally expensive Tag Heuer watch that had golden arms on a blue chronographic dial, showing his good time. He was clean shaven and wore cologne that gave his masculinity a sensual punch. His rugged good looks made him appear charmingly sophisticated. By his appearance, no one could make out that he could go to that extent as Lalu doubted. But Lalu had his own reasons. Although he had helped Lalu earn his first salary, but the one who had tipped Lalu about him and asked him to keep a check, could not be wrong. Lalu revered her. For she had not only saved his son's life, but had proved that she was a good soul.

When Chhotu had first complained of a severe ache in his abdomen, he had first admitted him at the private nursing home where he was employed. But instead of getting better, when his pain aggravated in seven days time, he shifted him to the famous government hospital. There Lalu met her. She had borne the entire cost of his treatment and stayed awake for three consecutive nights to bring him back from the clutches of death.

He and his wife had gone to thank her after their son was released from the local government hospital where she was treating him, and then she had said, "We doctors take an oath to protect our patients and give them the maximum priority in our lives. I have only abided by the oath that I have taken. So do not thank me, but thank your fate that he is still alive after he has been a victim of such a ghastly crime."

Right then Lalu was determined to help her resolve this case. It was his Chhotu's life that was played with. It was a personal vengeance that he sought now. This man had to be behind bars for what he had done.

CHAPTER 1

Piya unlocked the door while humming her favorite tune. She was in a brilliant mood.

As usual, she did not care to put the shoes back on the shoe-rack and threw her bright coloured college backpack on the study table before marching towards the bedroom. She opened the cupboard for taking out comfortable clothes to change into. She kept tugging at her tees and capris arbitrarily; unable to decide which one to wear, and suddenly, her diary caught her attention, peeping from the corner of the cupboard. Piya got glued to that diary, detailing her day right from the time she entered the class today, for she could not hold her excitement and wanted to express it somehow; anyhow.

Yes, that is Piya Roy for you. A simple looking girl rising up to an average height from the ground, with a thick bunch of long hair that spread across her back, which she mostly kept open; her oval face was beautified by big dreamy naturally kohl lined eyes, bordered with trimmed eyebrows arched perfectly, a small nose that gave her a childish look and a lip line that was neither too thick, nor too pursed. Overall she exuded an aura of audacity as well as bashfulness. She was simple to the core and appeared extremely lovable. She loved bright colours, simple ways of life and good food. She was loved by her friends and was a born leader. Everyone would run to her with their problems with a probable solution and she would take extreme pride in it and could give up her life to resolve those issues. She was fiercely protective about her friends and family. Anything could catch her fancy equally as fast as she would eventually lose interest in it! That is how she landed up renting this one Bedroom Hall Kitchen flat, a stone's throw distance from her college, where she lodged, instead of staying in the cheap 12' x 12' twin sharing hostel room. The small apartment was scarcely furnished with a single bed, a study table, a cupboard, a couple of chairs and basic kitchen amenities. The apartment was a few minutes' walk from the college hostel. What made it even a better place to dwell was that the owner was abroad and hence, there was no day to day interference regarding the apartment matters.

Her cell phone started playing Beethoven's Für Elisé which was set as her ringtone, bringing her back to reality with a jolt. "What Piya, where were you? I have been trying to call you for so long, but this phone of yours, just does not seem to get connected each time I call!" yelled Piya's mother. Piya was equally soft while responding. "Oh relax mom! In the tone that you are talking to me,

I can hear you even without a telephone", retorted Piya albeit politely, but cheekily! She always loved bantering with her mother. She actually missed her mom, whom, though she did not quite accept it openly, she considered her best friend. There was hardly anything she kept from her. Piya's parents stayed in Kolkata where her father was posted as a Senior Professor in the prestigious Government College of Economics. This was his last assignment before retirement and hence, her parents decided to set up home in Kolkata itself post retirement.

"You know how Bombay is Darling. We keep worrying about you. How many times do I tell you atleast give me a call once you reach home?" continued Piya's mother. But Piya's mind had already wandered off and she was a tad too restless to get back to her diary. She hurriedly made some excuses to pacify her anxious mother and kept the phone down and concentrated back on the diary, which chronicled how her life was shaping up.

Piya Roy was a normal middle class girl, hailing from a middle class family, but with a dream of making it big in life. Her father kept on getting transferred on his government teaching job and so her school kept changing, which is why probably she hardly had any close friends. After finishing her High School, she appeared for the Medical entrance examination and with the help of weekend classes that she had taken for a year, she easily cracked it. She wanted everything planned and organized in life. Maybe this is why she loved jotting down the daily happenings in her life very articulately in her diary! Infact writing was therapeutic for her. So, when she finally got through B.C.R. Medical College, a premier medical college in the newly sprouted portion of Bombay running across its coast line, she was more happy than worried about staying alone, away from her parents in a metro like Bombay. Initially she did take up the hostel accommodation but within a month, she started facing trouble adjusting to the food there and to the hostel warden. Her father then came and helped her settle down in the one BHK flat before leaving Bombay teary-eyed. Afterall, a father only knows best, how his heart aches to leave his little girl to uncertainty all by herself.

By the end of the first year, Piya's life was set. A private accommodation close to the campus, friends who she really gelled well with, a realistically good future and freedom from middle-class values – what more could she have asked for!

But something pained within. She could sit for hours with the 5″ x7″ photo frame, holding a pair of faces that she loved the most! She remembered clicking this picture of her parents during a Durga Puja outing, the most joyous celebration for every Bengali.

Piya was writing about Joy. Joy was her classmate whom she was best friends with since she joined college. He too was a single child, but bought up by a single parent. His mother had died when he was merely eight years old. Yet, he was an ever smiling lad. And Piya thought that he was her true friend. Many a times he had proved this to her in the past one year.

Today their first year results were out and she was overjoyed with her performance in the very first examination of her medical career. She went back in thoughts as she wrote how her day was.

She thought of the time when she was busy scanning through her grade card in the corridor when Joy startled her by yelling out her name.

"Hi Joy! Why are you sprinting??" Piya had said as she saw Joy running towards her yelling out her name.

"Hey Piya! Guess What? I managed to pass!" an excited Joy had exclaimed.

Piya loved this Joy. She loved his nature of being happy at the smallest of the small things. Nothing in this world could snatch away Joy's smile. He really lived up to the meaning of his name.

"Joy, breathe. I knew you would pass. What is so exciting about it? Now come on, show me your grades." Piya retorted.

"Listen Piya! Chuck the grades. The fact is I passed and it calls for celebration. Let us go to Mac Donald's and spend some time together."

"But we go dutch. Deal?"

"Deal it is."

Joy, though preferred paying the bill himself and hated going dutch, relented nevertheless. He at any cost wanted Piya's company. Piya was his best friend. Only best friend. And he loved spending time with her.

Joy bit into his filet-o-fish burger with extra mayonnaise and smacked his lips, "umm…yummy!" Piya tried hard to concentrate on her Grilled Chicken Royale and not have eye contact with Joy. She wondered why this boy always spent time with her, shared his joys only with her, but never spoke of his sorrow.

Piya had thought of Joy like this innumerable number of times in her mind. She wanted him to be hers completely; if not for seven lives, for one atleast; if not for a lifetime, for some years atleast; if not for some years, atleast for a moment. She could do anything; go to any extent, for Joy. For she loved him.

She asked, "So Mr. Sen, how much did you manage to score?"

Joy chomped down a bite and reluctantly replied "I barely managed to pass. I guess you better start giving me tuition now."

Piya was serious. She said, "If you are serious, I am ready. But no fooling around."

"I better not fool around with the class topper!" Joy winked.

They had finished off their meal and had lazily walked over to the pavement on the cross road. From here, Piya's apartment was barely half a minute walk to the left, and Joy's hostel accommodation, a minute's walk to the right.

Piya stopped writing her diary at this point in time. She wondered whether she should write about the grades, or about Joy. Then she decided against writing anything now and signed off. She got fresh, got into her sleeping suit and cuddled in bed with her copy of 'Partners' by Nora Roberts.

----x----

Back in Kolkata, Piya's dad was immersed in Kaushik Basu's 'An Economist's Miscellany' and her mother was watching a Bengali soap on Star Jalsha. Her mother commented during a commercial break, "What do you think is on with Piya these days? She is recoiling into a shell I suppose." He looked up to her from the gap between his brows and the spectacles hanging on the bridge of his nose, "You always read too much between the lines. She is growing. Do not eat into too much of her personal space. Let her be. I know my daughter. She will confide in us whenever she is in trouble." Her mother gave him a repugnant look and got back to her soap.

CHAPTER 2

Piya woke up to a beautiful Saturday on a chilly morning. Bombay was not cold even in December for people who hailed from East. Piya felt comfortable in this chill. The translucent white curtains dropping on the floor covering the French window to the east beamed bright when the rays of the first morning sun fell on them. She just looked at the curtains trembling in the light morning breeze like a bride on her first night. She cuddled up to her pillow and dug her small nose deeper into it. Pulling her quilt closer and tighter, she felt a tug at her heart and she wondered, *'Is this happiness? This early morning idyllic phase, having no worries about absolutely anything in this world, this feeling of completeness and satisfaction — this must be happiness.'*

But then, she was jolted back to reality by the buzzing alarm clock. By this time she was in the final year of her medicine course and was really stressed beyond limit. Getting through an internship, expressing her thoughts to Joy, Passing her exams with marks as per her parents' expectation, her next step in her career, too many things bothered her. And she wanted some respite.

She picked up her phone and dialed two. One was a speed dial to her voicemail, saved by default. Thereafter she had saved Joy's number on the first number available on speed dial. No answer. *'Joy must be sleeping.'* she thought. Then she thought for a moment and dialed him again. This time, after a very long interval, a muffled voice answered the call groggily "What is it Piya???!! Why are you such a big enemy of my sleep? This is the third Saturday in the last two months that you have woken me up so early!"

"Oh you were sleeping!"

"Obviously! Sane people usually sleep at night." Joy sounded sarcastic.

"Joy will you let me talk or keep on yelling?"

"Bark."

"Ok. Get up and get ready. We are going for a walk on marine drive."

"What? Do you even have the slightest of an idea how far Marine Drive is from Nerul?"

"I do. And I also know that you drive your bike pretty fast. So we are going for a morning walk on your bike."

"Oh God! Piya I hate you! Now keep the phone and let me get fresh." Joy could not say no to Piya. She was a cute little pest that he was used to by now.

Joy never had anyone who would at the least spend time with him, leave alone 'disturbing' him. Which is why he had grown so fond of Piya. He was a happy child till he grew up enough to sense a rising tension between his loving parents. Every evening was blotted with the din created by cheap fights that ended with the diminishing echo of his mother's sobs. He could never fathom why his mother was unhappy. All he knew was that even his father wanted to know what bothered her. He would hear noisy exchanges that would last for hours. His father would ask at the top of his voice, "Whatever I am doing is for you and Joy. I do not share my life with another woman. Why then do you not let me work in peace? Why are you so concerned about the way I earn? You are living your life luxuriously anyway. Why cannot you be happy with the fact that I came from nowhere and made a mark for myself and made you proud?"

He would hear his mother retort, "Because, I want you to sleep peacefully at night and because I want Joy to know when he grows up that his father was an honest and benevolent doctor."

"You are saying this because you are jealous of me. You are jealous that I became a renowned doctor in no time and you are still babysitting your days away." And thus, the argument continued.

Joy took refuge in shelves full of books. He detested his parent's fights as much as he loathed being alone in the room allotted to him. He gradually started withdrawing into a protective shell that he himself created around him through his reticence.

Life seemed to be quite uneventful for little Joy. He would often feign headache to ignore the pleas of his friends for a football match in the early evenings. For hours he would just not speak to anyone else, not even his mother. At times, in the lonesome nights, he would speak only to his 'buddy', which was a miniature of a Superman, who, as a child he thought, could solve all his problems.

But gradually, as he grew, his notion about Superman faded into oblivion. It was not that he was upset with his mother. It was just that he thought, probably the fights would end if his mother kept her mouth shut, and a diversion from what he thought was an ideal situation, irked him.

But he nevertheless loved her with all his heart. So when an eight year old Joy returned home from school to see his mother hanging from the ceiling fan using her own sari, he ran to her, holding on to her legs in the faint pursuit of saving her. Puzzled, scared, he ran to the phone kept in another corner of the same room. With shaky fingers, while still looking at his mother he picked up the cordless receiver and dialed his father's number only to be told he had left the hospital for an urgent meeting.

Pained, scarred, helpless, but diligently resolute in saving his mother, he dialed his maternal grandparents' residence. Although they arrived at a very short span of time, they could not wake up his mother from her eternal sleep. They were shocked. Too shocked to decide what is best. They tried taking away Joy from his father and in a fit of rage, lodged a police complaint against Joy's father. But he brainwashed Joy. Joy was told that his grandparents have snatched away his mother from him by not taking adequate steps when they came home to rescue his mother, and now were even trying to snatch away his father from him by taking him home with them and sending his father off to jail.

Little Joy's innocent and influenceable mind was easily moulded. He never again left his father's side. Gradually he learnt from his father that his mother was a selfish woman. Her own happiness was dearer to her than Joy's, which is why she left him and his father alone in this world. With this piece of information, he turned loyal to his father forever.

In the court battle, he stood against his maternal grandparents and that was a testimony good enough to acquit his father of all charges. Thereafter, Joy and his father were always there for each other, with each other.

----x----

Exactly twenty two minutes after Piya's conversation with Joy, they whizzed by on the Palm Beach road, which would shorten their hour long drive to Marine Drive.

At Marine Drive, Piya waited on the pavement while Joy parked his bike. She had rehearsed the dialogues in her head a number of times while coming here.

"Joy, why are we best friends?" Piya asked, as Joy jumped on the pavement while rotating his bike keys on his fore finger.

"Piya, why do you have to do this to me early in the morning? Why get so intellectual when we can be easy with each other? I mean, come on! We are best friends, period. What is the need to analyze and investigate the reason?"

Piya looked down. She had tried expressing her feelings to Joy innumerable number of times in the past but had failed miserably like she did just now. She just could not get to the second rehearsed line. Joy stopped her at the very first. Neither did she know how to explain this to Joy, nor did she want to keep it to herself. She nevertheless did not want to spoil this morning. So she just entwined her fingers into Joy's and kept on walking silently in the serenity of the early morning, not knowing quite for sure whether they both would be able to continue on life's journey like this forever.

Joy suddenly nudged Piya softly with his elbow, "Hey, are you upset with me?"

"No Joy. You know I can never be upset with you."

"Then what is bothering you Piya? I know you for the past one year and you are never so grave unless something is really bothering you hard."

"I was just worried about too many things."

"Like?"

"Like getting through an internship, passing the exam with flying colours, etc."

"Piya you know my father is one of the founder members and a Senior Doctor with the Bombay Medical School and Nursing Home. He can easily get us internships there. And it is I who should be worrying about such things, not you, because with the kind of marks that you score, worry does not suit you darling!"

"Then when can we meet Dr. Sen and talk about the internship? I can ask for his advice also on whether to do M.D. right away or work for few years before going in for my M.D."

"We can meet him any day we have an off. He is my father and has always had time for me whenever I have needed him; despite his busy schedule."

"Done then, you ask him if we can meet him on coming Tuesday. We have no lecture in the second half."

"Will do."

Piya thought how she could be closer to Joy for another year while doing her internship with him in his father's nursing home. Infact, she was decided that even if she bagged an internship in a topmost medical college of her choice, she would still do it with Dr. Sen; for Joy.

Piya at this moment could not think of life without Joy. Her universe revolved around him. But as much as her heart wanted to be his forever, just the way she wants him, her mind did not. Somewhere, the uncertainty of a prospective future together that came retrospect to Joy's demeanour scared her, made her uncomfortable in his presence. She unknowingly, retreated in a protective shell when with him. She did not want to be the one at the receiving end of a broken relationship. She would not be able to show her face to her parents then. No. Piya was determined not to let Joy know of her feelings for him.

They gradually strode back to where the bike was parked as a hectic day awaited them.

CHAPTER 3

It was 4 PM on Tuesday as Joy waited on his bike for Piya under her apartment. It would take them atleast an hour to reach Bombay Medical School and Nursing Home in Andheri, which was in the western part of Bombay.

This was the beauty of the city that Bombay was. It was divided in three long strips – the western line, central line and the harbour line. These bifurcations were along the railway tracks and ran almost parallel to each other. The harbour line ran across the coast, which was pretty close to the port and the sea. Nerul was one such station on the harbour line. The central line ran through the middle of Bombay and the western line ran through the most happening portion of Bombay. Andheri was somewhere towards the middle when one ran along the western line. However, if one wanted to travel from a station in the harbour line to one in the western line, there were very few trains that cut through the central line directly to connect the harbour and the western line at two stations. Else, one could drive down either via the western express highway on the western line, or the eastern express highway on the central line.

Joy steered towards the eastern express highway to cut onto the Andheri-Kurla Road from the highway, and reach Andheri on time.

"We should have left earlier. We might get caught in the evening traffic." Joy murmured.

"We will not get late."

"Yeah yeah, madam knows everything about Bombay roads, which is why she took so long to get ready!" Joy mocked.

"I don't like you." That was Piya's only ammunition against Joy when she knew she was wrong.

"Ok ok. Now stop distracting me and let me drive fast." With Joy saying that, Piya was lost in her thoughts again.

She wondered what Dr. Sen would say. Would he allow her to do her internship with him? How would he take her friendship with Joy? Then she thought to herself, whatever is in my destiny is going to happen. So why unnecessarily worry? Que sera sera – whatever will be will be!

At 5.30 PM, they knocked on the door with a nameplate that read – "Dr. Sudipto Sen, M.D., FRCS, London."

A man in his mid-fifties, bespectacled, slightly heavy with a light paunch, and an intelligent face with a receding hairline greeted them.

With the cursory glance that she stole of Dr. Sen, Piya found no resemblance in looks between him and Joy.

Joy hugged him "It is so good to see you Baba."

"It is good to see you too, son."

Piya touched his feet. "Oh let it be young girl. Come, take your seat and tell me what can I do for you? Oh before that, what would you both like to have?"

Joy's father, Dr. Sen, was a very liberal man. Joy had tipped him about Piya over the phone and he was more than happy to help his son and his best friend. He, by nature, did not like to read too much between the lines, and was naturally not quite interested to know whether they were much more than friends.

Piya on the other hand kept on gauging what could Dr. Sen be thinking, and in the process, got so engrossed in her thoughts that she forgot to reply to his question.

Joy nudged her, "Piya, I am going to have a chicken burger, what about you?"

"Nothing uncle. I have had a late lunch and do not want to feel stuffed."

"Atleast let me call for some tea, coffee or some cold drinks maybe, whichever you prefer. Afterall you have come here for the first time."

"Alright uncle, a cup of tea would do."

As Dr. Sen picked up the receiver of his desk phone and asked his secretary to get him two cups of tea and a chicken burger, Piya started wondering how Indians and especially Bengalis by nature were foodies and would never have a meeting without tea!

"So Piya, where are you from? What does your father do?"

These were generic questions that one asks. So did Dr. Sen to keep the conversation going. He was quite impressed by the fact that Piya's father was a Professor.

The tea came in sooner than expected, along with a plate full of cookies and a chicken burger for Joy.

Dr. Sen, as he passed on the cup to Piya, asked her "So Piya, tell me, what brings you here to meet a boring old doc?"

"Dr. Sen, I am looking forward to doing an internship with your nursing home so thought of approaching you with my testimonials directly."

"Hmm. I learn from Joy that you are a very bright student. So why Bombay Medical School and Nursing Home when you can easily get into the topmost government hospital or any nursing home for that matter?

"You are one of the most knowledgeable and successful doctors I have heard of, and I wish to learn from you and work under you." Piya hid the real reason behind her approaching Dr. Sen.

Dr. Sen was taken aback for a moment. He could not understand the reason, but he realized, the way Piya took care of Joy, the way Piya always stuck by his side, the way she was always an upright girl as much as he had heard about her from Joy, she reminded him of Joy's mother. And the word, "successful doctor", hit him hard in the heart. He knew how much his deceased wife detested his definition of success. She had always wanted him to be a dedicated doctor with no concern for money. But he wanted a luxurious life for his son and wife. He wanted fame at any cost. He wanted to earn so much money in a lifetime that it would not get over even in Joy's entire lifespan. And he did not feel even a wee bit repentant that he had to sacrifice his wife's life for that.

He was brought back to his chamber from his reminiscence by the 'hic' sound of Joy's bout of hiccups due to his rapid eating. He admonished him for his rapid eating habit and started thinking of Piya's question.

He thought and thought hard. He then suggested, "Look Piya, this country needs good doctors like you in the government hospitals and if you do your internship with us, you firstly reduce the chance of a government hospital having a good doctor like you and secondly, you reduce the chance of below-average students like Joy to get through an internship as the seats we have here are limited. So I think you should first give a try at one of the premier hospitals and in case you do not get through any, which i anyway doubt, then I would consider myself lucky to have you as an intern."

Piya's jaw dropped! "Ok Dr. Sen. I will do as you suggest. But please advise me whether I should go for my M.D. right away or continue working for a couple of years before doing my M.D.?"

"You are a star student Piya. But theory does not help alone. You should first gather some hands on experience with various patients and then do your M.D. that too preferably in a government hospital as the versatility of patients that you get there, will help you gather vast experience."

Joy was busy nibbling at his chicken burger. He interrupted their discussion at this point and asked "So Piya is not doing her internship here, right baba?"

"It is upto Piya, Joy. I have told her what I think. Now it is her decision. If she feels I am talking logic, she will agree. Else, as I said earlier, I would be more than happy to work with her."

"No Joy, I think Dr. Sen is right. I got to be practical, and think from the patients' point of view rather think for my own self." With that statement, Piya fell silent as she knew she had lost a chance to be with Joy for some more time.

CHAPTER 4

Joy was sweating profusely. He was sitting stiff with the question paper in his hand and was unable to answer even a single question. That sent a slight shiver down his spine. He frantically looked around for help. But no one appeared around. He kept on mumbling his prayers for atleast passing the medical test. Suddenly, out of the blue, Piya appeared and held him by his hand, and said, "Come with me. All your problems will be solved." He mumbled again. But this time, it was not the Gods he was naming, but was thanking Piya. Suddenly a massive push stunned him. He got up, sat on the ledge of what he thought was his college bench, only to realize that it was his bed and all along, he had been dreaming!

"Setu! What are you upto? Why did you hit me so hard?" yelled Joy while messaging his back with his bare hand.

"What am I upto? It is seriously a bad phase that the society is going through. Why else would you speak to me like that! Here I woke you up from your nightmare and you are cursing me instead of thanking me?" replied Joy's roommate Setu, aka Sethuraman sarcastically.

"What nightmare? How do you know I was in the midst of a nightmare?"

"Why else would you repeat Piya's name like that in your dreams? You generally remember her only when you are in trouble, right? You anyway claim not to be in love with her for dreaming of her, so I am sure it was not a dream but surely a nightmare!" winked Setu as he ran for his life after having teased him about the most sensitive topic of his life, while Joy followed him to level the scores.

Setu ran out to the street for fun knowing Joy would never follow him out in his shorts. Joy was way too meticulous about everything, including his dress sense, to do that.

He caught his breath while waiting for Setu to come back. Then he slowly walked back to his room thinking of what Setu had said.

Joy thought, *'Is this silly thing, love afterall?'*

He decided to brush-off these puerile thoughts and concentrate on his daily chores. But the thoughts kept coming back to his mind like the eternal waves of the sea that do not ever stop with the passage of time. He thought, probably, certain things continue to exist beyond the passage of time. Like his love for his mother. It was way more than a decade but he still craved her presence in his life. Piya was only the second woman in his life after his mother passed away. This subaltern gaze at life made him conclude that probably that is the reason he thinks so much about Piya and that he should immediately stop doing that and be more resolute in the mission of his life. To make it to a position in the society, which is, beyond what his father could. He would show him that he was his able son. He would prove to him that his father was right in putting all his faith in him.

Joy nurtured a secret wish in his heart which even his father did not know. He never expressed it to anyone. Which is why he kept to himself. Despite wanting to be normal like any other young adult, despite dying to fall in love and enjoy life, despite wanting to just forget all about his life's motto, he just could not. He as much as loved being carefree, his suddenly grown up mind did not allow him that luxury. So he appeared to be very carefree. As if there was nothing in this universe that could trouble him. And this showed in his attitude when he hung around with his friends. Even Piya could not understand the real Joy behind the masked Joy.

But Setu did. He always tried to cajole Joy to open up. He would often say to Joy, "There is something that troubles you always. Unless you speak about it, how are you ever going to solve it?" Joy would invariably laugh at him, "There is nothing in this world that can replace Joy with sorrow my dear friend. So stop creating ideas in your head."

When you stay with someone for long, you tend to become fond of that person beyond limit. Especially, if that other person is your friend in college and moreover your roommate, then the bond gets only better. Maybe, for this reason or for some reason best known to Setu, he had a special affinity towards Joy. He in some way, felt responsible towards him. He felt sympathetic towards this boy who had lost his mother at a tender age. He was a year senior to Joy and thought of him as his younger brother.

Setu hailed from a joint family in Chennai. The eldest of three children, he was not much missed back at home while he studied medicine at the BCR Medical College in Nerul, Navi Mumbai. His parents were always busy with his siblings as Setu was the more mature one among the three and his parents knew that he will be able to manage his show well. Setu did not mind. He was well content with his life. He did not need external motivation to keep going. Setu was more of a loving and giving kind of a boy. He expected less from others but gave more. He was never the class topper but once when in class eight, his father counseled him saying that children did not have any responsibility and that their parents did everything for them. Then why not put all their energy in excelling in studies?! That did the trick for Setu. He became way too serious about his studies and made a mark in his family by being the first one in his family to get through a medical college and a reputed one at that.

He enjoyed his time in college and particularly enjoyed his time spent with Joy. For Joy was otherwise a jolly good fellow and amused the ones surrounding him very much.

But something within him told him that Joy was not as happy as he appeared to be. And he genuinely wanted to help him. But did not know how to. The only thing he understood well was that Piya loved Joy but could not express well and Joy loved Piya too but did not understand that he did.

Whatever it is, Setu had left a trail of questions in Joy's naïve mind. He kept on wondering whether what he felt for Piya was love afterall, he kept on thinking, did love feel this silly, he kept on deliberating whether he had any place for love in his life. But the job was done by then. He had started feeling strongly for her.

Joy dialed Piya's number. "Hi, what are you doing for New Year's Eve?"

"Planning." pat came Piya's reply.

Joy did not waste a second in catching up with his next question, "And pray what are you planning?"

"Planning what to tell you when you finally make up your mind to spend some time with your so-called best friend on New Year's Eve."

"So-called??!! You think I just call you my best friend but actually do not consider so?" Joy sounded hurt.

"Well otherwise why would you not plan something out for New Year's Eve with me?"

"Hold on. I did not plan out anything for New Year's Eve with you? Why else would I call you asking your plan?" Joy this time sounded agitated.

"Firstly Joy, if you wanted to spend New Year's Eve with me, you would have decided and planned about it much earlier and secondly, if you had already planned, why did you ask me about my plan?" Piya childishly snarled.

And thus began another compassionate fight between two people who loved each other dearly but neither acknowledged nor displayed so, which invariably ended in the most dramatic and magnificent union followed by their own little celebration to glorify their friendship.

CHAPTER 5

Setu was busy observing Joy's dress for the night. Not that he had a great dress sense but still he was Joy's biggest critic and greatest ally. So whenever Joy was up to any important task, Setu was summoned to check whether Joy was up to the mark for the occasion.

"You are dressed perfectly for the occasion, brother." said Setu pulling up Joy's tee shirt slightly above his belt from within the denim jacket that he was wearing.

"And what do you think the occasion is brother?" asked Joy sarcastically.

"Why? Even a child knows it is New Year's Eve today!" Setu sounded a little peeved at being underestimated.

"Ha ha ha...there you go! I knew, only you could come up with such an expansive interpretation of the occasion!" This time Joy was peeved.

Setu, not knowing what to do or say, erupted like an active volcano that suddenly throws up ash, "Why would I not come up with this interpretation? Who except you knows your plans? I wonder if even Piya knows about it. Unless you tell me what are you up to today, do you expect me to see it in dreams how Joy and Piya are going to celebrate the New Year's Eve together?"

And Setu was stopped only by the bear hug that Joy used to take him into his embrace to cool him down. Though Joy wanted to tell him about his plans, he did not, lest the plan does not actualize. Because it was a very unique plan. He had tipped someone to make it happen and he was not sure whether he will turn up.

Just to pacify Setu he said, "At least you could have realized that I am going out with a girl for the first time and incidentally, you know the girl."

"Oh so that is creating butterflies in your tummy?" smiled Setu.

"No no I am fine. Absolutely." Joy tried sounding brave trying to suppress his anxiety over the uncertainty of the situation.

At the designated time, he picked up Piya on his motorbike and they sped off towards Thane, which was the main junction between the eastern part of Bombay and the central part of Bombay. From there on they moved towards the western part of Bombay via the Ghodbunder road so that they could reach the creek in the western part of Bombay where the sea took a marvelous turn to enter into the city like a bay where it was surrounded by the sea on one side and by land on three sides.

Once they reached there, Piya saw it was a dark alley off the main road ending in the creek water. There was not even a single soul in that enclosed area and that even if they needed help, there was nobody to help them. She was a little scared. But she was way too excited to feel the scare. She dismissed the thought and she shrieked, "Joy, we are going to spend the New Year here?" She did not know the exact plan. All she knew was that Joy had planned something different and that would surely please Piya. Piya was way too ecstatic with the fact that Joy had asked her out finally and she expected him to open up his heart this time. Everything put together, she did not question Joy about anything as she trusted him blindly.

Joy did not reply to Piya's shrieks. Instead, he kept on smiling and kept on tugging Piya towards the creek. Suddenly he stopped and excused himself to make a call. Piya was worried about his demeanour.

She picked up her ears and overheard him say, "Are you ready? Yes I too am here with her. Then come soon. We are waiting."

Piya suddenly felt a cold shiver run down her spine. She wondered had Joy changed his intention? Did he really not love her and had brought her here only for some sleazy behaviour? She, for a moment, deliberated running away. But she came here on the bike with Joy. How would she go? She would not find any public transport at this hour in the night. She was sweating heavily by now. Suddenly she was startled by a hand on her shoulder. She almost shrieked aloud when Joy's voice, suddenly suppressed, pacified her momentarily as she knew it was him. She thought as humane it is, when in trouble, human beings tend to trust the known though the known is not always the most trustworthy. She left it on destiny and followed Joy to where he led her.

In a moment, they were right next to the corridor which goes down towards the water that leads to a ferryboat. There she saw a boat. A wee boat with a thatched roof and a man with an oar in his hand beyond that roof. She was surprised. She looked up at Joy only to find him looking down, leading the way, holding her hand, careful enough not to slip on the moss laden path. She followed him in a trance.

Soon enough they were on the boat with no man in sight as the boatman was hidden from their view by the thatched roof. He was anyway facing the water with his back towards them and was oblivious to their presence. All that mattered to him was the money he got for this reserved ride.

The moment the oar hit the water, the splash sound of the water brought Piya back to her senses. She felt shy that she was staring at Joy all this time while Joy categorically avoided glancing at her. When the horizon started fading away in sight, partially due to the darkness of the night and partially because of the distance created by the boat moving away from the land, Piya realized a movement in the darkness inside the boat. A muffled noise of something being unwrapped. She wondered whether it was a gift that Joy had got for her. Then she heard a scratching sound; like the one when a matchstick is rubbed against a matchbox. And suddenly, the surrounding was all lit.

In that dim light she saw, Joy was holding a small muffin, with a small candle dug into it, lit, making the dark surrounding of the boat look grand at the backdrop of the dark sky. And just then, Joy touched his phone and Westlife's "You raise me up..." started playing in the background. She felt her heart skip a beat and her knees weak with the waves of surprises that came crashing towards her, one after the other, without giving her time to stand up against one.

In a minute, even before she could gather herself, Joy whispered, "Happy New Year sweetheart!"

Piya barely fumbled, "Happy New Year Joy!"

Then they both put off the candle, enjoyed the quiescence of the still night occasionally being drifted away by the splashing oar on the water, with only a few stars in the sky as witness, and simply enjoyed the moment that begun a new phase in their life along with the new year.

They both were quiet. Joy thinking, what lay ahead of them; and Piya wondering, was it a dream or the reality.

Piya felt a tug at her heart. She wanted to ask Joy what was happening, she wanted to know whether she had the entire night to her, to sit infront of Joy like this, she wanted to express her gratitude towards Joy to let him know how much she enjoyed this surprise. But she could not. They did not speak a word that night. Piya occasionally felt miserable thinking even if for a moment, she did doubt Joy when he brought her here and Joy did not even look at her in any untoward way, leave alone behaving sleazily. But she made up for that by just sitting close to him and taking in his presence with every breath of hers.

When back at the creek, mounted on the bike to get back to their respective homes, Piya finally managed to say, "Joy nobody ever did so much for me, to surprise me, to make me happy! How did you manage all that?"

Joy was thoroughly confused by now. He felt so strongly for Piya that he wanted to devote his entire life to her at this very moment. But his steadfastness for his mission, his wish, his desire for fame was stronger than the love he felt for Piya. He did not know how to express himself to Piya. He was a confused youth. He was a romantic at heart but did not want to come across as one. He loved her, but did not want her to know. And now that he saw the love light in Piya's eyes, he recoiled in a shell.

So he chose to portray what he did best. He just glanced at her through the rear view mirror on the bike and suddenly smiled his usual broad grin and said "I did nothing Piya, I just tipped the boatman to reserve his boat, met him earlier and kept the muffin and candle to surprise you and timed my mobile music player at 23:59 to start playing Westlife. Thereafter, I counted from sixty to zero so that it was New Year, when I wished you. Simple. You do not need rocket science to surprise somebody, moron.

Piya fell more in love with Joy for this demeanour of his. But at the same time, she was a tad disappointed that he did not propose to her yet.

Once Joy dropped Piya home in the wee hours of morning, she rushed inside, got fresh, made tea, called her parents to wish them a splendid new year and then ideated while sipping her tea sitting by the French window, how to make Joy express his feelings towards her. She had a lot of time before she got ready for college.

CHAPTER 6

The boy's hostel bustled with the fervour of young boys having fun at another's expense. Joy was being grilled like the turkey that is roasted on thanksgiving and surrounding him, enjoying the session thoroughly were Setu and team.

Joy had already described the entire night to them time and again but still had not been able to satiate their hunger to know more in details. He ultimately erupted like the volcano that sleeps for ages gathering enough heat to destroy lives in a moment.

"Should I now make up stories to tell you guys so that you stop torturing me?" he thundered.

That was a signal strong enough that he wanted to be left alone now. Setu signaled the others to keep quiet and himself moved away to his laptop to just let Joy be.

Joy turned around and fell asleep. Tired and spent, but satisfied, from the previous night.

"Hi!" Joy surprised Piya while she was sitting under the huge banyan tree in their college campus, busy nibbling on her small pack of snickers chocolate, her favourite.

Piya initially stiffened not knowing how to react to Joy after their last night's rendezvous, but soon enough eased, "Hey Joy! I thought you were sleep deprived and so would not be in college today."

Joy replied casually, "Yeah I was not planning to but I had to give you this gift so had to come! Saying this, he took out a small artificial rose, red in colour, sans any gift wrapping, that looked more like a box sitting on top of the green coloured stem, and held it out to Piya.

Piya was overwhelmed. She took it gracefully and felt her dream come true. She was ecstatic when Joy opened the top of the rose, which indeed was a box, and took out the adjustable ring fitted with a shining gem looking like a diamond. He put it on Piya's ring finger and smilingly said, again casually, "I will get you a real one once I start earning."

Piya could not believe her luck. She just hugged Joy and melted in his arms. Silence expressed much much more than mere words could have.

Life was beautiful for Piya. But Joy, on the contrary, was getting more and more confused about life. Neither did he want to ruin his mission, nor could he stay away from Piya. It seemed there was something about Piya that drew

Sukanya Sengupta

him to her. He went with the flow, but really got thinking hard one fine day. Joy felt strongly for Piya, loved spending time with her, but was not sure whether this was love. He did not want to get involved so much that he deviates from his focus. So he had kept his feelings under wraps from everyone including Piya. He had never told her that he loved her. Much so because he himself was not sure about it. So when Piya asked him one day whether they should speak about their relationship to their parents, he was taken aback. He did not know what to answer. He feigned a bad headache and returned to his hostel room to avoid her. Next day onward, he remained as normal with her as possible. He was very cool in his approach. No outsider could say they were in a relationship by Joy's demeanour. Piya was mature enough to notice that. But she was not so mature that she would gauge the reason. She took refuge in Rina, her very close friend in college, after Joy. Rina, being their classmate, knew both Joy and Piya well. She reasoned he did not love her. But Piya argued that she had felt it in his behaviour. She pestered Rina, "Tell me, why else would he take me out on New Year's Eve and gift me the diamond?"

"Piya! It was only an American Diamond. Not a real one." Rina sounded irritated at Piya's naivety.

"But Rina, he still gifted me, not someone else, and he took me out. What gift he gave is not important to me as long as he loves me." She reasoned.

Rina was a mature girl. She picked her friends after weighing out a lot of issues. She came from a not so well to do family and naturally, weighed out the pros and cons well before taking any decision. She did not want to break Piya's heart. But at the same time, she wanted to warn her of a possible heartbreak by trusting Joy so much. She tried pacifying her, "Piya it is only the inherent nature of boys. Joy is just trying to prove to you that he loves you. But he does not. Had he truly loved you, he would not be so cold towards you. Maybe he felt lonely on New Year's Eve and to assuage his loneliness he took you out and gifted you. If he truly loved you, he would not avoid you ever since the day you wanted to inform your respective parents about each other. He is reacting as if you have asked him to marry you."

"No Rina. My heart says he loves me. Only thing is I do not know how to make him express that!" Piya sighed.

Rina reasoned, "Look Piya, the way explicitly saying you love someone or making love frequently alone does not prove the sanctity of love, similarly, staying aloof and detached too does not. Love is something that you exude and your partner feels in your demeanour.

To me, people who say love is something that cannot be expressed do not understand what love is, or they have never felt Love. Love is something that will certainly ooze out if it exists. You do not need to work at it; you do not need to prove it; it just shows. And Joy's demeanour does not show at all that he loves you."

The next day when Piya met Joy, she was determined to find out what was there in Joy's mind. She told herself, *'No point in keeping false hopes. Today, either my heart will break or my life will be made.'* She put her chin up in the air and approached Joy.

"Hi Joy!" she casually said.

"Hey! What's up?" Joy sounded casual too.

"I want to ask you something. Can we talk now?"

Joy felt his stomach squeeze. He knew Piya was again going to raise that topic. He was determined not to let Piya know of his weakness for her. Mustering up courage, he casually said, "What is it Piya? You are sounding pretty serious!"

"Yes Joy I am and you too better be. I need to know NOW if you love me and want to spend your life with me. Tell me once Joy that you love me" Piya hit the point straight but her tough demeanour faded mid sentence. She could not be what she was not, with Joy.

Joy recoiled momentarily. He immediately realized he got to be stern in order for him to appear mentally strong. He very clearly said, "How many times do I express..." he paused a while and completed the sentence with tremendous mental strength, "...that I DO NOT love you!"

Piya was stunned. She did not say a word. Just walked away. When she saw Rina, she just ran to her and clung to her and the dam to her tears broke open. She cried her heart out. That was the first time she had tasted heartbreak. She was inconsolable. She simply sobbed and kept on repeating, "He does not love me. He does not want to spend his life with me."

This time, Rina sounded much soft. She made her understand like a mother does to her baby, "Stop chasing Joy. If you are destined to be together, you will be. He will come back to you from wherever he goes, however far he goes. You do not need to be behind him for that. But if you are not destined to be together, no force, natural or external can make him yours. So just follow the path of your life and leave everything to destiny."

This time, Piya took her words very seriously and promised to herself in her mind, '*from today onwards, Mr. Joy Sen, Piya Roy will not get hurt thinking of you.*'

Life went on as usual for Piya. Despite her promise to herself, she used to pine for Joy. Rina was her constant source of inspiration. Rina and Piya started getting closer to each other due to the growing distance between Joy and Piya. Rina used to deliberately spend more time at Piya's flat to keep her company.

Piya got to know Rina inside out. She started enjoying Rina's company. Especially for all the mature advice that she got from her. They started doing comparative study which helped them. What was the best thing of being friends with Rina was that they both being Bengali, they could spend hours chatting, sitting in Piya's flat, over a cup of tea and puffed rice, talking about Rina's small home at Kashimpur, a small village on the outskirts of West Bengal, which is about two hours drive from Kolkata. They spoke about how she and her two younger twin sisters, who were eight years her junior and still in school, snuggled under a single quilt, in the wintry nights of her village, how there would be no electricity for hours together and they would study in the light provided by dim oil lamps, and how she convinced her parents to go and stay in a city like Bombay, all alone. Piya would get Goosebumps listening to all the stories. She would imagine in her mind all that happened with Rina and feel how lucky she had been all through, never to be denied anything ever in life.

Joy on the other hand recoiled into a shell. He used to hate it when Setu checked with him about Piya. So Joy started distancing himself from Setu as well. He felt lonely. He missed his friends. After all he was only a twenty something lad. How much could he show off that was not the truth?!

CHAPTER 7

Piya and Joy both had successfully completed the Part two of their third year professional. Now, it was time for the one year compulsory internship. Joy did not even attempt to look out for internship elsewhere and directly joined his father's nursing home. Piya on the other hand had got a chance to intern at the famous SSKM government hospital.

Now they did not meet as often. Rather, they did not find enough time. But what none of them accepted quite openly was that none of them wanted to keep in touch that frequently or with as much fervour as they did when times were different. Piya however, had grown indifferent with Joy. She neither felt happiness, nor sadness in any of his behaviour. Joy had shifted back to his house in the posh seven bungalows area in Andheri and Piya continued at her rented apartment in Nerul as her hospital was near Chhatrapati Shivaji Terminus (CST), and she could easily commute by a direct train. Also, she could not afford a rented apartment anywhere near CST.

This distance was sure to harm their friendship. And Piya, though indifferent, had not outgrown Joy completely. So she would call Joy often. Irrespective of Joy's changing tone with time, she felt happy just hearing him talk.

Life went on as usual, busy for both of them until one morning, when Joy received a call from an ecstatic Piya.

"Guess what!" she exclaimed.

"I cannot. You say" retorted a busy Joy.

"You remember Rina? We are now interning together in SSKM."

"So?" barked Joy.

"She is getting married and has invited me over to come and stay with her family through the wedding at their familial home in Kashimpur, near Kolkata. She too is a Bengali and I would surely enjoy the Bengali rituals! I was anyway looking forward to a break so this invitation brings in some fresh air to my otherwise boring life!" Piya rattled off.

"Cool. Enjoy yourself."

"Joy! Are you not excited to hear this?" Piya sounded morose.

"Piya, you have got the invitation, not me! Nevertheless, go ahead, enjoy yourself and share your story with me once you are back." With this, Joy signed off.

Piya waited for a while sulking, wondering why did Joy not even ask her when is the wedding or when is she going to return. Then, remembering the days ahead chirpily got up and started making a to-do list lest she forgets anything!

She could not contain her excitement. She was ecstatic not only to be a part of Rina's wedding, but also to see her own parents after so long. Now the only task was to convince Senior Doctor at SSKM, Dr. Lad, her boss, for the leave.

Piya was a girl who could not concentrate on a single thing for long. While making the list, now she started worrying about Dr. Lad's reaction to her leave application and tossed the paper aside to get up and get ready for her hospital. As soon as she was ready, she did not even bother to have her regular breakfast of milk and cornflakes, and dashed at the door.

Though Dr. Lad was a gentle human being, he was not always as cool as the cucumber. Probably this nature of him bothered Piya. She kept on praying to God all through her journey in the 9:10 AM CST local.

Piya always travelled by this train ever since she started interning at SSKM hospital. It took her about an hour to CST by the train and then she walked down the pavement for a good fifteen minutes to reach SSKM five minutes before her scheduled time.

She generally listened to music on her way and did not have friends in the train. In Bombay it was customary to be friends with your fellow travelers, share food and seats, have fun together along the journey and carry on an endless chatter daily, without fail, without artifice. But Piya Roy was very choosy when it came to friendship. She had a sense of sobriety that bespoke class and taste; which is why her demeanour with Joy really surprised her own self.

But today, Piya was unable to concentrate on her favourite playlist playing on her phone. Her mind went adrift with the reaction of Dr. Lad that she envisaged. Unknowingly, she prepared herself for a tough day ahead.

On reaching SSKM, she headed straight for Dr. Lad's cabin and entered the lion's den with an anxious heart and greeted him with a meek "Good morning sir".

"Good morning Dr. Piya. Good you are here. I was just thinking of calling you regarding the Politician's health." Rattled off Dr. Lad the moment he saw her, inquiring about the local MLA who was admitted there for whom Piya was assisting Dr. Lad.

"Sir, he is doing quite well and can be discharged today. But what worries me is the child's health who is admitted in the neo-natal unit with a congenital heart dysfunction" said Piya defiantly forgetting all about the leave issue momentarily.

Dr. Lad smiled and said, "You are taking care of the child well, are you not little lady? Do I really need to worry about it when I have such a big paediatrician in the making, right here in my hospital?

Piya felt slightly relaxed at this faith that Dr. Lad bestowed on her. Then she utilized this moment to place ahead of him, the leave issue with her lips curled up in a smile, "No sir I am quite confident that the child will pull along. It is now only a matter of time. I am only hurrying because you know Rina's wedding is just around the corner and I wish to go visit my parents and enjoy her wedding as well. But not until the child has been cured completely. And I am sure you will grant me the leave if he gets well soon."

Dr. Lad's reaction was unexpected. "Rina's wedding? Who Rina?"

Piya chuckled at this. "Sir I am referring to Dr. Rina who, like me, is also interning here and is getting married in Kolkata on the eighteenth of next month."

"18th of next month? That is just around the corner! Well fine, since you have decided to go, go ahead. But make sure you handover the cases well for the days you are not here."

Piya did a little jig in her mind and prepared to run to Dr. Rina to break this news to her while she trailed off with an ecstatic "thank you sir".

CHAPTER 8

Tring tring rang the landline phone in the living room of Prof. Roy's residence in Kolkata. Mrs. Rupa Roy was busy smearing the perfectly cut pieces of hilsa fish with mustard paste, readying them for the traditional Bengali dish 'ilish bhapa'. The tring tring distracted her. She unenthusiastically washed her hands and while wiping them on the long trailing end of her sari, strolled towards the cordless while grumbling, "God knows who is it at this odd hour".

She casually hollered, "Hello…who is this?"

A muffled female voice replied, "Your daughter has been kidnapped!"

Before the voice could say a single thing more, she started howling crazily uttering Piya's name time and again.

The voice again spoke, this time, much clearer, "Oh god ma! You spoilt all my fun by this hue and cry! How I thought I would give you a surprise!"

Mrs. Roy was still unsure as she spoke, "Hello…..is it Piya? Are you sure you are Piya? Or are you the kidnapper making a fool of me?"

This time Piya burst out laughing at her ma's naïveté, "Ma….how I wish I could just hug you tight now, right at this moment! How can you be so cute! I was just making some fun. I am no kidnapper and besides, who dare touches your daughter?"

A naturally worried mother replied, forgetting all about her ilish bhapa, "No child, you do not know this big, bad and ugly world yet. Nevertheless, leave all this for the moment and tell me how did you come to call me at this hour today? All ok with you?

Piya could not contain her excitement, "Ma please ask Baba to take a leave on the fifteenth of the coming month, and be there with him at the Howrah station at five thirty in the morning sharp. I cannot wait to see you guys".

Tears welled up in Mrs. Roy's eyes. She was going to see her daughter after almost four years. "We cannot either Piya. Love you. See you soon." was her curt reply while trying to sound normal.

In her excitement, she had forgotten to ask her the reason for her visit, how long was she going to be there, and also how could she manage such a sudden leave.

In the evening, once Prof. Roy arrived, she blurted excitely, "You know our Piya is coming home on the fifteenth. She has asked you to take a leave from college that day so that we can go pick her up from the station."

"Piya is coming? Suddenly? What has happened? And why leave? Is she not coming by the Jyaneshwari Express that reaches in the wee hours of morning? That way, I can pick her up and head for college after dropping her home." Came an anxious stream of questions from Prof. Roy.

"Good lord! Give me some time to reply atleast! When you ask questions, you never give the opponent a chance to respond." retorted Mrs. Roy curtly.

"Ok ok now give me all the details." Prof. Roy sounded anxious.

"Even I do not know all details. In my excitement, I forgot to ask her all these." Mrs. Roy sounded so naive at this moment. She waited a while before she continued again. "All I know is that she will arrive at Howrah Station at five thirty in the morning on the fifteenth and we have to go pick her up. And since she wants you to take a leave, I am sure she wants to spend some time with you after so many years so for her sake atleast I feel you could take a leave." calmly replied his obedient but otherwise controlling wife.

"You are sounding as if I do not want to spend any time with my little princess! You remember Rupa, when I first saw her, the doctor said Goddess Lakshmi has adorned your home! How happy we were! Especially I. Piya had indeed filled this home with love and laughter…"

Picking up the trail from where Prof. Roy breathed, Mrs. Roy dreamily carried on the conversation "…and you remember how she used to throw tantrums that she will only eat out of your plate and be fed by you when you sat down to have your food before going to college?"

"How she used to pester me for anything ranging from a big teddy bear to a bicycle to a Maruti 800 instead of a Fiat Padmini when we went to buy our first car!"

"Do not blame my Piya. You only enjoyed her tantrums and satisfied each one of her demands despite our meager means." chided Mrs. Roy.

Prof. Roy laughed out loud at this and replied happily, "You are in a way right Rupa. I always felt Piya is lucky for me and meeting all her demands was one way of showing my love and gratefulness to her.

Mrs. Roy suddenly mellowed down and wiped a droplet from her left eye "How our little princess has grown! And so big that in a few days she will fill someone else's home with love and laughter and all we will be left out with will be her childhood memories…"

Prof. Roy blared, "I am not going to get my daughter married now. You dare not hammer all these in her head right now."

Mrs. Roy responded with only a blend of a sharp and sad look this time, probably for not knowing what to say as she herself was not yet in a frame of mind for getting Piya hitched.

CHAPTER 9

The train whizzed past platforms, the names of which could not be read; entering into tracks that passed through golden paddy fields hued red by the molten radiance of the rising sun. Autumn had waved goodbye and it was that part of the season when the chill in the air sent shivers of fondness all over the skin.

Piya jumped down from the upper berth and peeped out of the window just to feel the breeze of her homeland on her face. The wind slapping against her cheeks felt like her beloved mother's palm tracing the edge of her face. She almost choked with emotion and wondered if she missed her family so much now, how would she ever stay away from them all her life post marriage?

Gathering herself up, she hurried to get fresh and arrange her belongings that she used in the train, before she could finally be with her parents, muttering to herself all the while about the delay in the scheduled arrival time.

As the train rumbled to a halt at Howrah Station few minutes before 6.30 AM, Piya jumped off with the only backpack she was carrying; her expectant eyes scanning the crowd for the 5 feet 11 inch lean frame whom she revered the most in the world.

Instead she spotted the short and stout innocent looking lady with shades of grey around her ears desperately looking for her in the crowd. She retraced her route and approached her from the rear planning to surprise her. But a light pat on her shoulder surprised her instead!

She turned around to find her father broadly smiling at her. "Baba!" She exclaimed as she threw herself at his broad chest and just started crying, unabashed.

Prof. Roy hugged her tight enough to just make her feel how much he missed his little girl in all this while. But verbally he kept on pacifying her saying "Piya come on, let us go and meet your mother. She is waiting."

They both waded through the crowd to where Mrs. Roy was perspiring in such a comfortably chilly morning wondering where Piya and her father were. The moment she saw them approaching, in her anxiety, she blurted "Already the train is running an hour late, and look at you two! No worries for me. Father – daughter duo enjoying each other's company God knows where!"

While Prof. Roy tried reasoning, Piya just ran to her and clung to her, digging her nose deep into her neck and taking in the scent of her mother, which was not a scent of any deodorant spray or any perfume, but the earthy scent she only got from her mother's body! Something she associated with petrichor - the scent of rain soaked earth.

Prof. Roy hurried "Let us go now Piya, you have had a long journey. Let us get going. Have to pick up something for breakfast as well, knowing you will not let go of your mother easily now."

Piya and Mrs. Roy sat themselves at the rear seat while Prof. Roy occupied the passenger seat in front hurling route instructions to his college driver who was doubling up for the Roys' personal driver by ferrying them from the station to home.

The driver switched on the car radio and the popular Bengali patriotic song *'dhanadhannye pushpe bhora'*, by Dwijendralal Ray, filled the car with an exquisitely rich melody. Piya did not utter a word, her eyes turned moist and she thought to herself, *'this song is such an epitome of a lyrical masterpiece; why on earth then did this song not get selected as our National Anthem?'*

She just rolled down the window, and stuck her head out. She could feel the breeze blow over her face. Durga Puja was just round the corner and the white perennial kans grass, fondly called *'kanshphool'* in Bengal, swaying in the same breeze against a backdrop of pure blue sky was adding to the aesthetic feel of the same. Piya wondered how will it be enjoying Durga Puja at home again with her parents after so many years. She quickly started mentally planning as to how she would squeeze in Rina's wedding and Durga Puja all together in her mere fifteen day break.

Prof. Roy's voice startled her, "So Piya, would you now like to throw in some light on your trip details, or do you wish to reach home first, get fresh and then tell us."

That embarrassed Piya. It was not as if she did not want to give them the details, it was just that she wanted to surprise them and moreover, she herself was not sure about the finer details of her trip. So she arbitrarily replied, "Baba, it is just that it was like an era that I did not see you and ma. So when Dr. Rina, a friend from my medical college and now a fellow intern, invited me over for her wedding, I jumped at the idea and made this program impromptu. That way I thought I will be able to spend Durga Puja too with you both. Since nothing yet is fully planned, I do not yet have a return ticket booked. Let us go home, sit together and finalize everything. What say ma?"

Prof. Roy beamed with pride at this. He did not wait a second to pull an upper hand on his wife in this regard, "Did I not tell you that our Piya did not take a single decision without our consent?"

Mrs. Rupa Roy knew her husband well. She smilingly said, "The vantage is always yours I know!"

Piya enjoyed all these. She was at her calmest when she experienced solitude being amidst her parents' causerie. Her favourite pastime being, lying down between her parents, with her head on her mother's lap and her foot on her father's, idling, with the conversation buzzing in her ears, but she not listening to a word of it.

On the way the Roys picked up some *samosas* and *jalebis* for breakfast and reached home well in time for a round of chatter at the breakfast table. There was enough time for lunch. Mrs. Rupa Roy was a brilliant cook and managed her time well. She kept everything ready beforehand so that the cooking time was minimized. Hence, she was pretty relaxed at ten in the morning as she knew, even if she entered the kitchen at eleven or eleven thirty, she would be done by the time Piya and Prof. Roy would be ready after bath.

"Piya!" yelled Mrs. Roy from the open kitchen.

"Yes ma...I am ready." responded Piya coming out of her room in her lounge wear. She was ready after bath. Ready to gorge on the finest, albeit according to her, culinary creation that made her salivate even when she was full to the brim. She laid the table and waited for her father to come and occupy the space at the head of the table.

She was particularly fond of fish, especially if it was cooked by her mother in Bengali style curry. So the mere thought that she was going to savour fish curry prepared by her mother after so many years, kept her occupied since morning, ever since they finished breakfast. But one more thought too kept her busy since morning - that of the Durga Puja.

As soon as Prof. Roy sat down for his lunch, even before Mrs. Roy came out of the kitchen to serve them food, he asked in a high pitched tone, so what is for lunch today? Have you prepared all of Piya's favourite dishes? But Piya was not interested in discussing food at that moment. She somewhere deep down felt that her Puja celebration was going to be different this year and yet wanted to go out somewhere with her parents during the Puja. So she wanted to be doubly sure about her parent's plans. She digressed, "Baba, what are your and ma's plans for Durga Puja?"

Prof. Roy was a serious old man. He did not like speaking more than required and kept mostly to himself. He loved Piya unconditionally and to him, enjoying Piya's company meant sitting with her, having their meals together, fishing together, reading together, but never chatting together. He particularly did not like speaking much while having his meals. So when Piya asked him about his Durga Puja plans, he grimly replied, "I thought we were going to discuss not our but your Puja plans so that you can accommodate Dr. Rina's wedding and Durga Puja in this fifteen day break."

Piya glanced at her mother and said, "Exactly. That is why I first asked you if you and ma have some plans because, if you still do not have any plans, then we can make some nice plans maybe visit some nearby place or do something different this Puja."

Prof. Roy cut her short mid way.

"I believe you have come all the way from Bombay to Kolkata to enjoy Durga Puja here and we should spend it here in Kolkata itself. I and your ma never make exclusive plans for Puja except for the fact that we visit the Puja Pandal of our colony to pay our homage to Goddess Durga each morning of the four days that Goddess Durga stays here. So this year shall be no different. You go ahead and make your plans."

Piya was expecting this reply. Mrs. Rupa Roy was silent all this while. She felt from within that Piya probably wanted to go out with them during the Puja as it was a fun festival for all Bengalis and Piya was still a young girl who could have a different definition of fun in her mind. Moreover, she thought, *'How many more years that our Piya will stay with us! Who knows she might get married in a different city and might not be able to spend Durga Puja again with us!'*

This thought created turmoil in her mind and she blurted out, "Why do you think that since we enjoy going to our colony pandal every year, even she will enjoy that? She is grown up now, she might feel like going pandal hopping in the city, or probably she wants a different celebration. Why do you not let Piya decide this year?"

"Rupa, I know she is grown up, which is why I know she will not enjoy pandal hopping with us. Let her go and enjoy with her friends. And let us enjoy the way we do. What say Piya?" reasoned Prof. Roy.

Piya simply said, "Ok, let Dr. Rina's wedding get over on the twentieth. Then I will plan if at all I want to do anything; as it is Durga Puja starts only on the twenty third."

"And what will you do on the days when there is no wedding and no Puja?" caringly asked Mrs. Roy.

"I will get loved and pampered by you Ma! God knows when next I will get the chance." Piya suddenly turned nostalgic.

CHAPTER 10

It was already the early evening of 18th of October.

The hall was bustling with positive vibes all around. The wedding ceremony was just about to begin. Piya was stuck by the side of Dr. Rina.

Piya was decked up in a light sky blue zardosi sari studded with white stones, and a thin platinum earring and necklace set studded with a light sky blue stone each. She was sans make up but wore a light shade of lipstick and a thin line of eyeliner. She looked elegantly graceful. She looked so pretty that Dr. Rina teased her, "You are looking so pretty that I am afraid my groom might reject me for you". Piya chuckled and eased out next to her colleague cum good friend.

She was very happy today. She could not say why but it was as if happiness was in the air and she could sense that something positive was going to happen. She kept on waiting for the wedding rituals to begin with bated breath.

Exactly at dusk, the wide framed man with a tuft of hair on the backside of his otherwise shaven head started chanting Vedic verses creating an enchanting environment. The bride and the groom sat side by side and repeated the same with fervour. Just then, her eyes met his. They both exchanged a polite smile that is typical of strangers and carried on with the ceremony.

After the first day of the wedding ceremony was over, when the bride was surrounded by all her cousins, Piya being the only friend of Dr. Rina from Bombay, she was all by herself and did not know anybody else there. Naturally, she felt left out and gradually wandered off to the buffet counter. While scanning the menu there she saw him again.

This time, the stranger walked up to her and in a very husky, manly tone, simply said, "Hi".

He was about 5 feet 10 inches tall, but his straight posture made him appear a couple of inches taller. He was extremely fair, had a rectangular face, a straight lip line and deep black eyes. His thin brows were shaped into a deceivingly perfect arch and were joined at the centre. His thick mop of black hair was cropped short. He was lean but broad shouldered and held his face forward in a steady gaze that gave him an air of authority that was discernable. Piya found him handsome.

"Hi" repeated the stranger startling Piya out of her reverie.

"Umm...hi!" Piya sounded slightly nervous.

"Well, I am Abir. Abir Ray. The groom's childhood buddy."

"And I am Piya. Piya Roy, the bride's colleague."

"Aah! A doctor! Nice to meet you doc."

"Same here." was Piya's curt reply.

Piya could sense her heart throb. So she moved ahead in the pretext of checking out the dishes, lest she blabbers something incoherent that undermines her self respect.

"Ahem ahem." he cleared his throat to draw her attention.

With this Piya looked back again, startled.

"I hardly know anybody of my age here except for the groom who is incidentally busy getting married now and I think you too are not known to many here so I was wondering if we could chat while eating. Do you mind if I join you?"

Piya was visibly interested. But she maintained a composed demeanour, "But I hardly know you Mr. Ray."

"We infact would not unless we speak to each other madam. And moreover, can we not simply stick to Abir and Piya instead of Dr. Roy and Mr. Ray? For god's sake, we are at a friend's wedding and not at some godforsaken corporate party." he sounded slightly peeved this time.

Piya was transfixed by his throw of words. It was not as if she was not interested but she did not know how to open up to a stranger so easily. She kept on thinking while he expectantly stared at her.

When his stare could not elicit an answer from her, this time, he mellowed down a bit. "Look madam if you are not comfortable speaking to me or addressing me by my first name, fine. I mean, I am no rogue. I am a journalist by profession and I do not have any negative history behind me. So it is not as if I am trying to demean you. I genuinely am feeling out of place. And I felt the same about you. So thought we could help abate each other's boredom. But in case you are not comfortable, please carry on, I would not bother you." With this, he started walking away, feeling his self respect impaired for the first time.

"Abir please wait."

Abir stopped midway and turned around to find Piya smiling at him.

"Whenever someone takes longer to get to know you, always remember it does not mean that person is not interested to know you. Instead, it means that the person is trying to know you better and deeper."

"Well now I guess you know that I have zero experience when it comes to girls and reading their minds!" winked Abir.

Piya felt happy to have met someone who is sober enough for her to chat for the rest of the occasion.

"So Piya would you like to eat something first and then maybe we can just chat over coffee?"

Piya was as it is famished. So she eagerly grabbed at this idea. Sitting together, they ate to their heart's content and casually walked over to the terrace while being submerged in sharing minutest of details about their lives, with each other.

He held her attention with the story of his transition from a petty reporter to an eminent journalist.

She made him laugh with the story of her journey from being her baba's little girl to a grown up doctor.

He enchanted her with his grandeur.

She charmed him with her simplicity.

And that was the beginning of a grand bonding.

----x----

It was the morning of the twenty third, the first day of Durga Puja.

Piya was up and about early that day. She had made no plans whatsoever in the last three days and kept on thinking, for some unknown reason, about Abir, whenever she was not in a conversation with her parents.

She spoke less. Her mother wondered what had got on her, seeing the ever so talkative Piya so silent. Her father was happy that at last Piya learnt to speak only relevant stuff and not keep on blabbering the whole day.

Piya was sitting with her parents in the local Puja Pandal when her phone vibrated. Since they were in front of Goddess Durga, she had turned her phone onto vibrate mode lest the sound distracted the priest.

She looked at her screen and a smile flashed through her face.

"Who is it?" Mrs. Roy asked casually.

Piya did not answer her mother. Still smiling, she simply strode over to the exit and walked over to the nearby banyan tree that stood alongside the canopy. She walked as if she was in a trance.

"Hey what a pleasant surprise!" Piya sounded happy as she received the call.

"Surprise?! I thought you would be expecting my call. Remember I had taken your number on the day of Arun's reception." Abir smilingly said in his manly tone.

"Well I hardly know you so how could I have known whether you would call or not. I thought you might have forgotten all about me." Piya chided in a complaining tone, making it very clear that she had been expecting his call and that he should have called earlier.

"My apologies for not spending enough time with you to let you judge me well madam. May I compensate for my behaviour by taking this opportunity to ask you out?" Abir was as manly in his demeanour as he was good with words.

No woman could say no to the way Abir asked her out. So Piya relented, though she felt the way Abir was talking, was quite unlike him. He did not appear that flattering when they had met at Dr. Rina's wedding. Nevertheless, they decided to go pandal hopping to the city's best Puja marquees those were slated to win the top slot in various categories in the best Pandal competition that took place in the city.

After Piya came back to where she was seated, she started wondering how to tell her parents that she is going out with a boy, alone. It helped when Mrs. Roy turned inquisitive. She simply replied, "Oh ma it was an old friend, and we are planning to go and see some idols tomorrow. Should we?"

That 'should we' part did the trick. Prof. Roy and Mrs. Roy both loved the fact that Piya did not do anything against their wish and hence, at once they expressed their consent.

----x----

"Hey!" waved Abir when he saw Piya come out from the metro station.

They had decided to take the metro rail to the farthest instead of driving down to avoid the traffic and then come backwards via metro again as they hopped from one canopy to another.

"*Shubho Shoshthi*!" Piya wished Abir.

That was the first day of Durga Puja and that is how one was expected to greet others on that day. It was the sixth day after '*Mahalaya*' and hence the word '*Shoshthi*'.

They caught up on some general chit chat and went ahead in the crowd.

Occasionally the back of Piya's hand brushed Abir's in the crowd. None of them expressed anything, but it did send shivers down both their spines. It affected them both. No they were not lovers, but felt good in each other's company.

One thing that Piya definitely noticed and enjoyed was Abir's protectiveness. Each time somebody would come bang in front of Piya, Abir's broad frame would shield her like armour. She felt safe and happy in his presence.

After a while, they went to a nearby coffee shop, tired of standing in the queue to view Goddess Durga. They ordered cold coffees with ice cream and sandwiches. Piya noticed, their food habits were just the same and their choices matched. Abir and Piya spoke for a while discussing the remaining days of the Puja.

As soon as the food arrived, they gorged like crazy. Then having satiated their hunger, they walked over to the nearest pandal and continued on their pandal hopping spree.

Around evening, Piya said, "It has been long Abir. I am tired. Moreover, I got to go now, lest I get late. I want to reach home before it is dark."

Abir simply looked at her, said nothing, and just stared at her. Piya understood that he did not feel like letting her go. But Abir was silent. He suddenly said, "let us go" and started walking back towards the nearest metro station so that they could take the metro back home.

Piya felt bad but could not help it. She then realized that even she enjoyed spending time with him.

Piya had never been out alone with a boy barring a couple of times that she went out with Joy. She kept on comparing her moments spent with Joy with the moments that she spent now. She realized, with Joy, she was merely enjoying. But with Abir, she was really living each moment.

She said nothing. For she did not know what Abir felt for her. But something within her stirred. The similarities between them, his words, and his presence, all felt surreal to her and she felt probably, if not her life partner, he could be her ideal soul mate.

CHAPTER 11

Abir switched off the bedside lamp in an attempt to sleep. But sleep repulsed him.

He tossed, turned, woke up and walked to the kitchen. Drank up half a bottle of water and instead of walking to his room, walked straight to his parents' room.

Abir's parents never bolted the bedroom door at night. He walked up to his mother's side of the bed and called out to her softly, but nevertheless, waking her up.

She sensed something and softly whispered, "Do you want me to go to your room and talk?"

Abir nodded and they both strolled over to his bedroom.

Abir made his mother sit on the edge of his bed and rested his head on her lap, sighing.

Mrs. Gita Ray knew her son's pulse well. She put a hand on his head and softly said, "Tell me what is bothering you son. I may not be able to solve your problem but it will certainly alleviate your mental turmoil."

"Nothing serious ma. You know I attended Arun's wedding; there I met Piya. She is Arun's wife's friend. I just wanted to talk to you about her."

"Hmm. Piya. Isn't Arun's wife a doctor?"

"Yes ma."

"So Piya too is a doctor?"

"Yes ma. But how does that matter? I mean whether she is a doctor or a gymnast is secondary...."

"Then what is primary Abir?" trailed his mother.

"Ma we got along well during the wedding, exchanged numbers, went out during the Durga Puja and have been in constant touch ever since over phone. But in the past six months, I have started feeling for her differently and that is causing me a lot of stress."

"Well so it is a pure case of one sided love, is it?"

"Ma had it been so, I would still not be so restless. But I do not even know if this is one sided or both sided. I rather do not know what she feels for me or thinks of me. In fact I am not even able to speak to her freely due to an innate inhibition, and I do not know what is this state of inertia that has gripped my being."

"Do you think of her often?"

"Yes I do."

"What do you think of her as a human being?"

"Ma I do not think much substance. All I know is that I am happy in her presence, virtual or real."

"Hmm. Where does she stay?"

"Bombay. There she is interning at the SSKM Government Hospital."

"Ok. Connect me to her tomorrow. I will speak to her."

"About what? You are going to speak to her about my insomnia? Ma you are crazy!"

"Not as much as you are Abir. Now try to sleep a bit. You are looking sick." saying this she put her palm on his thick mop of hair, wondering what would be the right way to approach this matter.

Abir enjoyed his mother's warmth and company and in a little while fell asleep with his head on her lap.

Since childhood Abir was very very attached to his parents. Unlike other kids his age, he would sleep between his parents even when he was old enough to shave. And when he finally started sleeping in his own bedroom, his parents got into the habit of not bolting the bedroom door.

He grew up in a joint family and only recently had they started staying separately in the flat his father purchased at Newtown in Kolkata, with the retirement money.

When he first made up his mind to study journalism, his engineer father was extremely unhappy about the fact that despite such good grades Abir was not willing to sit for the joint entrance examination for engineering and medical. But his mother had that belief in him that his indomitable spirit would help him endure the rigors of a pioneer life of a struggling journalist. And she was right.

Abir was very active and was always interested in outdoor sports, mostly football. He was an ardent follower of the local Kolkata club 'East Bengal' and nothing could stop him from going to the ground to watch East Bengal take up their Arch Rivals 'Mohun Bagan'. But Abir was never seen with women. He would run away with an excuse each time he was introduced to some damsel in some party.

He would rather watch some old football match than go out on a date on his off days.

So given the boyish nature of Abir, it was very difficult for Mrs. Gita Ray to digest that Abir was probably in love with a woman who did not love him back.

CHAPTER 12

Piya was an early riser. But she was not figure conscious. But something within her had changed of late and so she had got into the habit of jogging early morning since the last couple of months.

Infact she had noticed a lot of changes within her in the last couple of months. Out of which, she was most bothered about her affinity towards Abir and her arctic relation with her once best friend Joy.

But the distance between Piya and Joy had not soured her relation with him. She still used to call him, but the frequency of calls had reduced substantially. However, her heart did not warm up to him as it used to be. Piya's dream of being with him always as his wife and taking care of him in the role of his deceased mother, besides being his wife had turned futile. Maybe Joy did not want it. It pained her. Especially when spring adorned the air with love.

On one such spring morning, she was preparing to leave for her jog when her cell beeped. It was a message from Abir saying "Hi! Want to introduce you to Ma. Let me know what would be a good time for you to speak peacefully on the phone."

Instead of typing a reply, she dialed Abir.

"Hi! You are quick!" Abir sounded happy to have received her call instantly.

"Hmm. That I am." she gagged, instantly adding "Hey but all ok? I mean why suddenly you want to introduce me to aunty? Is she listening to us speaking?"

"No dear. She is busy making tea in the kitchen. Last night we had a chat about you and I promised her that I will make her speak to you so while she went to make tea, I thought let me check with you what would be a good time for you to speak to her." Abir finished in one breath.

"Oh but what chat?" Piya sounded nervous.

Abir quipped, "Relax! You are acting as if I told her I am marrying you."

Instantly Piya stopped. Something stirred within her. She sat down and started thinking about what Abir had just said. Was this really a joke? Or was Abir serious? Would she really mind? What about Joy? She stopped thinking at this point and got back to her senses. She could then hear Abir holler her name checking if she was there on the line or had the phone got disconnected.

"No no I am very much there Abir. Sorry. Say what were you saying."

"I did not say anything when you were thinking Piya. I last spoke when you heard me alright."

Piya was embarrassed at this. Abir knowing her state of mind had indeed flustered her.

She somehow gained composure. Just then Abir said earnestly, "Ma is here. Would you like to talk to her now?"

Piya immediately felt her stomach all in knots. Though she was not yet mentally ready to speak to Abir's mother, out rightly denying speaking to her in front of her would sound demeaning so she reluctantly agreed. "Yes please pass her the phone." she simply said.

"Hi Piya."

"Hello aunty. How are you doing?"

"I am happy that my son has started befriending girls nowadays." chuckled Mrs. Ray.

Her ears turned red. "Aunty we actually met at Dr. Rina's wedding and I am sure Abir must have told you the details of our meeting." said Piya nervously.

"Yes darling but what he did not or rather could not tell me is that to what extent do you both like each other. So let me be very frank with you Piya. Tell me what do you think of him."

Abir kept on expressing his disapproval through muted animations but Mrs. Ray was determined to cure her son's insomnia.

Piya was dumbstruck. Nevertheless she replied, "Aunty I am doing my internship now and hence, am not concentrating on anything else at this moment. I am sure my father has his own plans for me."

And that did the trick. Mrs. Gita Ray knew that very moment, that her surmise was not incorrect.

She knew Piya was not against marrying Abir but was not sure enough to take it forward naturally being a girl.

"Piya if you do not mind, can you help me with your father's contact number?"

Though Piya hesitated for a moment, still she finally gave in courtesy sake. Mrs. Ray repeated the number aloud after Piya while Abir jotted it down in his mobile phone.

Mrs. Ray handed over the phone to Abir saying, "I am done. Do you want to speak to Piya or should I hang up?"

Abir was flabbergasted. He just took the phone and spoke in a very low voice though his mother had left the room. "Piya I am sorry. I did not know what ma was going to talk to you about. Infact this is possibly the only case in the whole wide world where a boy's mother talks about his feelings to a girl. Gosh! It sounds crazy!"

Piya did not know whether to be nervous or to feel happy about it. She simply managed some courage and blabbered, "Abir are you serious? I mean do you really think you want to marry me? We just know each other for the last 6 months and have not met more than thrice!"

Abir admitted he liked her beyond a simple friendly fondness and said in a hushed tone, "Even if you do not have any feelings for me, just let ma speak to your father. Afterall, you would eventually marry of his choice, so what if he likes me!"

He continued in a heavy tone after a brief pause, "Piya, should you never fall in love with me, I promise you that my love would be enough to keep us both happy!"

Tears of happiness welled up in Piya's eyes and a sudden longing for Abir welled up in her heart. She knew she had fallen for him.

The next day, Mrs. Gita Ray called Prof. Roy and fixed up a meeting at the Roy residence.

The two sets of parents met and Mr. Ray briefed Piya's father about the occurrences in the last couple of months, continuing, "Prof. Roy, so what do you have to say about this?"

Prof. Roy was dumbfounded. He had not even in his wildest of dreams thought that Piya could fall in love and keep that a secret. So all he could manage to say was "Let me speak to Piya and get back to you Mr. Ray."

After Piya clarified everything over the phone, detailing each situation to them, being the understanding type, they calmed down. Prof. Roy simply sighed, "Indeed our Piya has grown up Rupa."

After much discussion and deliberation from both sides of parents, it was decided, that Piya and Abir will be married by next spring.

CHAPTER 13

Joy was in midst of nothing when his mobile phone beeped. He was simply throwing instructions to one of the ward boys at his father's nursing home where he was gradually getting at the helm.

"What a pleasant surprise! How come you remembered me suddenly? Is there something I can do for you?" answered Joy.

"No Joy. There is actually nothing that you can do for me. And I did not remember you suddenly. I reminisce about you more often than you do." It pained Piya to reply to Joy like that.

"Well madam, I take back my words. Ok let me put it this way, this is your first call to me in the past six to seven months. So I was wondering what made you call me out of the blue."

Piya could not believe Joy could speak to her like that. It pained her to feel that he was not happy to have received her call. She was not sure whether Joy complained as she did not call for so long or had he completely changed? This uncertainty helped her to be sure of her feelings. Now she was convinced that she did not want joy, but peace of mind. And with this deliberation, the first thought that stuck her was that she was engaged to be married to the man who loved her beyond her expectations.

And that was important. In an era where nobody loves another without a reason, Piya felt she was lucky to have got Abir and his love.

"Hello! Piya would you like to say something or have you called just to hear my voice?" carped an audibly irritated Joy.

This was not the Joy she was looking for. She silently replied, "It seems you are busy Joy. I better call you when you are free. Let me know a convenient time for you to talk."

Joy felt a tinge of regret at this. He did not mean to hurt Piya. He had just turned indifferent towards anything that was not related to his nursing home business anymore. He quickly collected himself up and added, "Piya I am sorry. Please do not think like that. You certainly called for something important. Please tell me what is it."

She simply replied, "Joy I am getting hitched next spring."

Joy gaped. Not that he was unhappy but slightly taken aback at this sudden statement. He did not intend to get married to Piya anytime soon but still had some feelings left to feel happy at the fact that she was going to be someone else's soon.

"So will you not meet me once and give me details about your wedding? When do I get to meet the lucky one?"

Piya thought about this for a moment. She had thought he would never again meet Joy after this conversation. But something within her told her that she ought to introduce Abir to Joy. Possibly she wanted Joy to see what a man Abir was so she casually said, "Abir is expected in Bombay next month. I can make him speak with you then."

Their conversation ended after a short exchange of few casual statements.

Just after seven days, she received a package at home. She was surprised. It was a small box gift wrapped carefully in red. Once the delivery man was gone, she sat cross legged on her bed opening up the gift wrapping carefully. She did not like tearing off wrapping papers as she felt all gifts were wrapped with extreme care and should be given the due respect. Once she was almost done opening the wrapping, she saw a small little red jewellery box peeping from inside the wrap. She extracted it carefully to see that it was a solitaire inside with a warranty card, which meant it was a real diamond. Her heart thumped faster.

She smiled thinking how romantic Abir was. Then, she saw a small white card attached beneath the ring holder inside the box. She opened it hurriedly to read what had he written. It read –

"I had promised to gift you a real one once I started earning. Sorry for being slightly late. But this only befits the occasion. Congratulations in advance on your wedding."

Piya was shocked! She realized it was not Abir who sent her the gift but Joy. The day when Joy had gifted her the American diamond passed by in front of her eyes. She remembered how the next day he had said that he does not love her. She did not wish to keep it. For a moment she deliberated returning it. But thought it would not be courteous to do so. She kept it, but vowed never to wear it.

A month passed in a jiffy. It was time for Abir's visit to Bombay. He had not met Piya after their marriage was finalized. Hence, this short trip.

Piya was waiting at the arrivals in a white cotton top and blue denim. Her hair was left lose and was tucked under her glares that she had lifted up on her head. She wore no makeup except for a natural shade of lipstick and a floral fragrance.

Her expectant eyes were searching the known frame amidst the passengers flocking out of the exit. Suddenly she spotted him. Their eyes met yet again.

Abir was mesmerized by her simple yet gracefully elegant looks.

He came out hurriedly with a duffle bag thrown on his shoulders and instantly hugged Piya and planted a kiss on her forehead.

Piya melted in his arms. She felt weak at her knees. She looked into his eyes and simply said, "I missed you."

Abir, in his deep manly voice barely managed to say, "Let me take you home once. I will never again give you an opportunity to miss me. I promise."

Then they made a dash at the gate hoping to reach the office guest house that Abir had booked for himself, soon.

Piya, ever since her college days had stayed alone in the small rented one bedroom flat, and hence, it was ruled out that Abir would stay in her flat before marriage considering they both had a conservative middle class upbringing.

It was decided, Abir would stay for three days. Though Piya was least interested in introducing Joy to Abir after the ring incidence, she relented as she had already briefed Abir about Joy as her classmate and once a best friend. Abir had reluctantly agreed to meet her best friend once. If now she backed out, Abir might think differently. So they decided to meet and that too at the same Mac Donald's where Joy and Piya frequented as fellow medical students.

They met at the decided place and time on the first day itself.

After the casual introductions, they settled down and ordered some cold coffee to beat the summer heat and some light snacks to go with it. Abir was at his best with Joy, joking occasionally about Piya. He gracefully asked him, "Tell me how was she as a student, what all were she interested in, I mean I just want to know everything about her." Joy thought for a while and just said, "Piya was the life of the entire batch. Whoever had any issues ran to her for a solution, including me." Joy laughed. Abir continued with the laughter, "Must be! After all you do not get such beauty with brains combination often, do you?" Their casual conversation did not last long. Piya too did not speak much but all along she kept on wondering how life changes. She had never thought she would be sitting at the same place with Joy, as mere friends, introducing him to her fiancé. She reminisced about the day their first year results were out. That was the first time Joy and Piya had visited this Mac Donald's together, without their usual group of friends.

Three days passed faster than she expected. What impressed her the most about Abir was that he was not at all carnally inclined towards her. This was a very rare trait in men these days.

As Piya bade goodbye to Abir, she hugged him and whispered, "Do not go please..."

He replied, "Just three more months..."

CHAPTER 14

The indigo flight carrying a full load of passengers touched base at Kolkata exactly at 10.25 AM on Sunday, the first of February. Piya unbuckled the seat belt even before the 'unfasten seatbelt' sign was turned off. She hurriedly paused the music playing on her mobile and switched off the flight mode. The first call she made, was to her father. Now with their wedding barely a month away, Abir was not expected to come to receive her at the airport as per traditional Bengali customs. Amongst all the travel bustle, Piya remembered the last time she came to Kolkata. Each and every scene played in her mind like cinema. She felt so nostalgic that she almost cried!

She was in a relaxed mood now that her internship was over. Piya was now a full-fledged doctor though she had not joined any hospital yet. It was now time for her to get hitched.

Her mother, Mrs. Rupa Roy ensured to give her home made ayurvedic pastes for her skin and hair everyday, which she thought would make Piya have a glowing skin and shiny hair. What she did not realize was that the love Piya felt in her heart was enough to give her that glow.

Gradually, a month passed amidst a great brouhaha for the grand wedding.

In a blink, it was the 2nd of March. It was a bright sunny morning with a silver lining behind every cloud and a singing cuckoo adorning every tree. Flowers were in full bloom and spring was in full swing. For Piya and Abir, love was in the air.

Guests kept swarming Piya's home since a day before. The morning madness continued as the females of the house remained busy with the rituals. Piya's father remained busy with the priest. Piya was surrounded by her friends. Dr. Rina came over a day in advance though her husband, Arun stayed back to accompany Abir in the groom's car. Dr. Rina and Arun kept on taking credit for this wedding as Piya and Abir had first met at their wedding.

The bustle continued till evening when they all finally got ready for the actual wedding ceremony.

Piya was waiting at the venue for Abir to arrive. She looked glamorous in a bright red coloured zardosi banarasi silk sari. She was covered in gold ornaments. A traditional thermocol crown called the *'mukut'* adorned the frontal portion of her head. She wore a bright red *'bindi'* right in the middle of her forehead. Her face was bedecked with dots made of sandalwood paste starting from her brows, right upto her cheeks.

She emanated an aura of surreal divinity.

Abir arrived amidst the pure sound of blowing conch shells and holy ululation.

He was dressed in a golden kurta and a red dhoti with a golden border and the traditional *'topor'*, which is a conical headgear made of thermocol that is worn by the groom during traditional Bengali weddings.

The *'muhurat'* or *'lagna'* – the auspicious moment, in which the wedding vows are taken, was decided to be *'godhuli'*, which means the dust that flies in the crisp evening air following the retracing steps of the cowherd that returns home; implying dusk. While the day converted into the evening at dusk, Piya Roy, amidst smeared vermilion, chants of Vedic verses and sacrifice of ghee into the holy fire officially became Mrs. Piya Ray which transformed her from an audacious lass to a bashful bride in an instant.

Next day was the *'vidaai'*. Piya officially, socially and legally, had to bid adieu to her parents and proceed with her new life, to her new home. She remembered the day she left home to study medicine in Bombay. She had cried her heart out that day. But today, her own tears despised her though her heart heaved from pain.

She threw back a bowl of rice grain from top of her head, indicating as per the Bengali tradition that the bride repaid all the debts to her parents for whatever they did for her in her lifetime. And this is when she realized that she was leaving her parents, forever. She broke down like a wailing child. Her parents could not get her back to her senses. It was then that Abir stepped in.

He came forward, held Piya by her shoulder, and said to her, "Do not cry thinking your parents lost a daughter today. Smile knowing they gained a son." As Piya looked at him astonished at his grandeur, he repeated, "Yes Piya. I mean it." With a pause he continued, "From today onwards, my parents are your responsibility and yours, mine." Then he looked at her parents and said, "I know the uncertainty you are going through right now. But trust me, if there is anyone alive in this world who has loved Piya, possibly not as much as you do, but with everything that he has, it is me. So come what may, I shall stay true to the vows I have taken with the holy fire as the witness."

After this assurance, Piya still cried. Not in pain, but in happiness.

Abir's mother waited at the door to greet them. And as Piya and Abir stepped in after completing the rituals there, Piya winked at her saying "Thank you and thank you". Mrs. Gita Ray smiled and asked, surprised, "A double thank you for what??" Piya simply said, "The first one for giving birth to a son like Abir and the second one for bringing him into my life." Mrs. Ray's eyes shone with tears of happiness. She hugged both Abir and Piya together, making her small world complete as Mr. Ray looked on fondly.

The day after, that is the third day of the wedding was the reception arranged by the groom's side and called '*boubhaat*'.

Piya wore a golden coloured lehenga with golden thread work and heavy junk jewellery to go with it. All this, was gifted to her by her mother-in-law. She wore light make up giving her a divine look. All the relatives flocking to catch a glimpse of her appreciated her candid demeanour as much as they cherished the gala reception.

That night was their first night together. As Abir shut the door, he whispered, "So Mrs. Piya Ray, how do you feel?"

Piya teased him back, "I feel I am on seventh heaven. Why do you not pinch me to make me believe it is all true?!"

Abir came forward and lightly planted a peck on her cheek and said, "Reserve the pinching for later; for now, I guess this is enough." and they both shared a hearty laugh on this.

As they both changed into comfortable night gears, they casually started chatting about their honeymoon. While Piya wanted an elaborate and exotic one, Abir, under pressure from his workplace to join back soon, wanted a quiet, virgin place, which would not take them long. That was their first discord.

However, they sorted it out concluding, both the party's interest was paramount and after much deliberation, they concluded that they would honeymoon at Saba - an unspoiled queen of the Caribbean, which is a potentially active volcano on Mount Scenery, ranging barely 13 square kilometres in area on the Caribbean islands.

It was a beautiful place to be and to cherish their togetherness.

They decided they will fly directly from St. Maarten island to Saba's Juancho E. Yrausquin Airport as besides rum and lobster, this island was famous for its airport, which was one of the riskiest in the world - because, it had the shortest commercial runway in the world.

They spent the rest of the night reminiscing together about how they met, came together and fell in love. They sang together, a Bengali song, *"Ke prothom kachhe eshechhi…"* the first few lines of which translates to, "who among us first came closer, who among us first stared, we really cannot decide, who among us first fell in love…"

On the second day after the reception, they were to return to Piya's father's place as a couple for a ritual called *'dwiraagaman'*. Usually that lasts for two and a half days but Abir and Piya, being time crunched, shortened it by a day and a half to fly away on their honeymoon.

On the designated day, they packed their backpacks and duffles, and set off for the isle of women.

When they landed in Saba, Abir was astounded. He was a person who would study any place that he was visiting, thoroughly. And so it came naturally to him when he told Piya not taking his eyes off the horizon, "Look Piya, Saba's morning is really as elegant as the meaning of its name!" Piya was equally amazed at the beauty of the isle. While having her eyes transfixed on the beauty of the place she asked, "What is the meaning Abir?"

"Beautiful morning."

"Abir you research so well about a place! Please sketch up an itinerary for our stay." She kept on pestering Abir.

"Do not worry sweetheart. You have me with you anyway!" Replied a smiling Abir as Piya rested her head on his responsible shoulders. She loved it. She loved being taken care of like a baby. She loved being protected just the way Abir did. She was living every moment of her life to the fullest.

They walked hand in hand on the damp soil of Saba, through the ferns and the mango trees...and through the 800 steps carved from stone that reach from 'Ladder Bay' to the settlement known as 'The Bottom'.

The unspoilt natural charm of Saba brought them closer mentally, much more than they were.

The next few days whizzed past sightseeing and visiting the Elfin Forest Reserve, Mount Scenery, Saba's prime fishing ground and the Wesleyan Church.

They enjoyed themselves with the naivety of children while scuba diving and hiking.

Driving the narrow strip of land called "The Road" is considered to be a daunting task there, with extremely difficult curves to maneuver. But they hired a car and Abir took Piya on a long drive on The Road. While Abir drove there with great élan, Piya clutched his sleeves tightly muttering to herself under her breath nervously.

Then Abir took Piya to the Saba University School of Medicine, a prime educational attraction there, and Piya, fell all over in love with him again.

Their 7 day trip was filled with a collage of memories, enough to last them a lifetime.

Their whirlwind honeymoon got over too soon. While Piya lamented for more, Abir had to balance work as well. However, to make their honeymoon extra special, he arranged for a return via the ferry service through the sea back to St. Maarten from where they flew back home, craving for home made food.

CHAPTER 15

Life went on as usual for Piya and Abir. It was autumn already and by now they were settled in their new home, their very own home.

It was a plush two bedroom apartment facing the south eastern portion of the hemisphere at Newtown itself, closer to Abir's parental home. Abir was always very attached to his parents. But they needed their own privacy and space and moreover, Abir wanted to invest in a property to save the huge amount of income tax that he had to pay.

While studying medicine, Piya had already got used to staying alone and so, did not mind staying away from her in-laws. She loved to decorate her house her way.

She bought similar long lacy white curtains for her home that once she used to have in her accommodation at Navi Mumbai.

Their home was adorned with a variety of potted plants ranging from the Jade plant to the Peperomia and the English Ivy to the Spider plant. The corridors were lined with similar looking white squared pots holding 4 Snake plants. Peace lilies were placed next to the white leather sofa in her living room.

But she loved the Heart-Leaf Philodendron the most, for two reasons. Firstly, it made its way down from her bookshelf and secondly, because of its perky, dark green heart shaped leaves, which reminded her how much she loved Abir and her books. Overall, the theme of the house was pure white. Peace was at every corner of the house.

But Piya at times wondered, was she really at peace with herself? There was nothing that she lacked. With Abir, she was happy beyond her expectation. They went out for dinner quite often, holding hands through busy roads. They danced merrily at discotheques. They cried together watching love stories made into movies. They lived life to the fullest. But somewhere, Piya was not at peace with herself.

It was just the two of them at home. On a lucky day when Abir returned home early from work, they would sit together with cups of coffee in hand and simply chat. She would often tell Abir, "I at times wonder what I would just do when I grow old enough to get tired of treating patients!"

Abir nonchalantly replied, "Why? I am sure you are going to have our kids to spend time with. Plus, I do not plan to die soon. So you will have even me for company!"

"Stop joking all the time Abir. I am thinking of the scenario when we turn empty nesters. And as far as you are concerned, I do not plan to chat with you like this all my life. Anyway you come home pretty late. Nevertheless, how much can we talk Abir? As it is at the rate at which we converse, we are hardly going to have any topic left to discuss on." Piya retorted.

Abir just smiled, shrugged his shoulders and simply said, "So you think this much is enough?"

Piya was confused. She mumbled for the lack of a valid answer which she did not have for this sudden twist in the tale. "I do not understand what do you mean." She finally managed to say.

Abir then stoically replied, "I think the more you love to engage in a conversation with someone, the more likely are you to live happily forever with that person, because when you grow old, when you have nobody to spend time with or nothing to do, when your eyes are too weary to read and when your ears are too hollow to hear, the person whom you love to converse with will keep you company, simply chatting, sharing your space and by just being there quietly by your side."

Piya thought for a while and said, "And what would we do when we have an argument? I will not even have my ma to share my problems with. It is going to be so lonely for me!"

Abir casually dragged on, "Well, I do not think I can manage much in this regard. So let me clarify one thing that I can confirm, that I shall never cause any argument."

Abir was way too chilled. He did not have any complain about the way his life had shaped up. He had loving parents to guide him, he had a lovely wife to love him, he was the owner of such a beautiful house and recently he was promoted at work as well. Life was all set for him.

Abir had always been an above average meritorious student. Naturally after passing his journalism, he easily got campus placed at the India Times, one of India's leading print media companies.

Needless to say, he got promoted faster than usual and naturally was burdened with additional responsibility, way too much for his age. But he enjoyed this adulation at work. He took it upon himself to prove that the only journalist the top management thought of in case of a serious breaking news was Abir Ray.

Abir was climbing the corporate ladder fast. He kept busy with social media too often and too long these days as his new assignment demanded so. Consequentially, he became more and more detached in familial matters and started depending on Piya for smallest of small things pertaining to their home or personal life. Initially she enjoyed this adulation.

Piya had not joined any hospital yet. She was not sure whether to go ahead with her Masters first or to get attached to a hospital and gain some experience first. She took time adjusting to her new lifestyle. Moreover, Abir's detachment had started to brew a storm in her mind and everything put together, she gradually drifted towards a deluge of abstraction that threatened to destroy her peace haven someday.

She felt she was possibly bored. But she reasoned with herself that possibly more than boredom, it was the lack of independence that disturbed her peace of mind.

She started getting eccentric. Initially not with Abir, but gradually, even with him.

Gradually their relationship was slipping away from their hands.

Abir lead a simple and modest life but was no jerk to ignore his wife's predicament. He deliberated hard on it. One fine morning, to make things better, he left home with the idea of coming back with two movie tickets, to surprise Piya. But a rigorous day at work deterred him to do so. Rather, he was late beyond imagination that day.

He rang the doorbell in the night, eagerly waiting to clarify to her his predicament. But when the door opened, he was in for a shock.

Mrs. Gita Ray, and not Piya, opened the door and without even exchanging a greeting, ushered Abir to their bedroom. He was aghast seeing an unconscious Piya lying listless on their king sized bed.

"Ma what is wrong with Piya? What has happened to her?"

"She would not be any better with your words of sympathy" came a rude answer from his otherwise composed mother.

"Atleast tell me what is wrong with her? Has a doctor attended to her? How did you know she is unwell?" Abir rattled off.

"I called her in the morning casually just to check on her and she sounded indisposed. So I just came over with some food thinking we can eat our lunch together and that way I can tend to her if she is unwell. But I did not expect to see her like this. By the time I came, she was almost unconscious with high fever. I called your father immediately and he got a doctor. Now she is better but she needs tending for a while. As usual you are late. You go and sleep in the other bedroom, let me sleep with her tonight." His mother sounded firm.

Abir could not deny his mother anything. He, like an obedient child, dragged his feet to the adjacent room. But sleep eluded him. He kept on wondering why suddenly Piya fell sick. Was his inattention towards her the reason? He started thinking of the day when like this he was unable to sleep and then his mother had taken it upon herself to demystify his relationship with Piya. Thinking hard about Piya, he did not realize when he fell asleep.

When he woke up, the sun had come up bright and birds were chirping happily on every tree. He pushed the curtains apart and drew in a breath of fresh air telling himself, "*This is it. Today onwards, I am going to take care of my Piya. I will not let anything harm her. Nothing should come between us. Not even my job.*"

And he rushed to check how was Piya doing. She was sitting up reclining on a pillow with the support of the bed stand and sipping on a mug of warm milk. His mother sat across her. He simply walked in and his mother left the room almost immediately in the pretext of getting him some tea. She knew they needed sometime together now.

Piya looked frail. Abir just hugged her tight and in a mushy tone said, "Next time you are upset with me, dare you not fall sick. You just punish me for everything. Do not punish yourself." Piya hugged him back and in an instant, forgot all about her angst.

Abir took an off to be with her that day. In the afternoon, after a hearty meal cooked by his mother, he lay Piya down and slowly started explaining things to her.

He said, "Look Piya, challenges are an inherent part of any relationship. Every relationship requires time to evolve. And as it evolves, we change. Change here does not mean we become a better person. Change here means we adapt more comfortably to the relationship, and in turn with one another. And then we break through the shell of our small self that constraints our lives. I am no marriage counselor to counsel you but I am an ordinary man who loves his wife very very much to lose her to such estrangement."

Then he dug his nose deep onto her shoulder and simply sighed; their closeness assuaging his inner pain.

Piya did not say a word. Abir probed, "Come on Piya, do not remain silent. I know you better than you do. So do not hide anything from me. Tell me what is bothering you?"

Piya felt accountable to Abir and decided to reveal her state of mind to him. She told him what exactly she felt.

Abir listened to her patiently. He suggested Piya to go for her MD in Medicine and hence, get attached to a hospital.

Piya generally took Abir's advice seriously. And the time was right. She got herself registered and started preparing for the All India Post Graduate Medical Entrance Exam (AIPGMEE) for that very year, which was to be conducted in the first week of December.

Piya kept busy with her preparations and Abir, after work, took good care of her. Abir at times prepared a strong cup of coffee when Piya was busy revising her notes and they shared a casual moment with each other. They both were happy. But Piya was worried. She wondered whether she will be among the lucky few who cleared the AIPGMEE at one go. But Abir kept her motivated. She felt lucky.

Soon enough, it was December, the time for Piya's exam. She wrote the exam very sincerely and hoped to get Paediatrics as her major. Once the exam was over, Piya felt a lot unburdened. She became a lot more stress-free and happier.

In a flash it was mid January. On the date of Piya's result, she first went to her in-laws place early in the morning and sought their blessings. Before she could leave home, Mrs. Gita Ray, who loved her like her own child, fed her a spoonful of homemade curd, mixed with sugar, which was considered to bring in good luck.

She then scooted off all excited, with Abir in tow.

Piya was excited to know about her fate. When she reached the venue, lo and behold, she had topped the list from her college. She felt a lump of joy form in her throat. She felt like jumping in sheer joy and hugging Abir but she could not. Instead, she only nursed the lump formed in her throat. Such was her nature. She could never enjoy in a vehement manner. But for a fleeting moment she thought of Joy. She thought of the day when their first year results were out and she thought of the Mac Donald's outing all at once. She immediately gathered herself and called her mother first. And then, after an emotional outburst, she dialed her mother-in-law; all this while, wondering why did she even care as much about Joy now that he did not seem to bother at all. And moreover, she was in a fairytale marriage with Abir and had no qualms whatsoever. She nevertheless thought of calling him once later in the day.

Piya after getting back home, hurriedly got fresh, and jumped on her cozy king size bed. Then after much digging, she extracted her phone from her handbag and dialed Joy. It rang exactly seven times. No answer. She knew the kind of a person that Joy was; he would not put his mobile phone on silent mode, so the fact that he could not hear the phone ring was ruled out. Moreover, Joy was one person, who picked up the phone at one go even when he was with patients, whenever someone close to him called. And this was the first time that Joy did not take Piya's call.

Piya was slightly dismayed. She nevertheless decided to wait for Joy to call back.

But the call never came.

Days passed into months. Piya got into the groove. She was already making her presence felt as a doctor. Abir kept on encouraging her to attend Medical conferences whenever possible to upgrade her skills. And she always paid heed to Abir's advice.

Since the day of her post graduation entrance exam results, her life changed in both perceptible and subtle ways, acquiring the hue of a working woman, and a doctor at that, besides being the understanding wife and obedient daughter that she had been all along.

CHAPTER 16

Piya was busy packing her bags. She had her clothes, books, shoes and papers all lying untidy next to her.

It was barely a few months that her MD course was over. She was going to attend a medical conference on organ transplants. This also involved neo natal cases and hence, she was super excited. This was one of the most critical aspects of infant treatment and she was looking forward to it. As usual, she was humming her favourite tune, which came naturally to her whenever she was in a happy mood.

Abir was bored flipping through one of Piya's Nora Roberts books that cluttered their bed while Piya was busy packing. Romance did not gel well with him when it came to his reading habits. He was more of an Agatha Christie and Jeffrey Archer fan and was intently in love with resolving crimes. Just to draw Piya's attention, he casually said, "So wifey, you are all excited to visit Bombay again?" Piya replied with a smile on her lips, "Yes hubby.

That I am. After all I am going to learn about so many exciting cases!"

Abir was enamoured by her sheer presence. He joked, "Please ensure that you only solve cases. Do not fall for some handsome doctor there."

Piya's smile vanished in a while. She got on her feet, went to Abir, hugged him tight and just said, "Never again joke like that Abir. I cannot think of anyone else other than you. Leave alone falling for someone else."

Abir felt proud at this. He felt euphoric about Piya with time. He wondered, *'How can this woman love me so much? Do I indeed deserve all this love?'* But he held a steady demeanour and teased Piya saying "Do not worry Madam. Even if you like someone else, I will escort you out of the relationship like your knight in shining armour." Saying this they both rolled on the floor sharing a hearty laugh about it.

Amidst all the joke Abir casually mentioned to Piya, "You know, I am one of the contenders to the post of a Senior Reporter in the special crime branch. That position is based out of Bombay. Who knows we might have to shift base to Bombay soon and you might have to pack your bags yet again!"

"Wow! And you are mentioning it to me like this? Why did you not tell me earlier Abir?" Piya said lovingly.

Abir was always chilled. He smartly said, "Relax Piya. You are behaving as if I am already on my way to Bombay! I said I am only a contender. As it is my boss does not want to release me as he is way too dependent on me. So let us just wait and watch!"

"Luck be with you Abir."

"You are my lucky charm Piya. Ever since you have stepped into my life, things have turned only for the better."

"No Abir. It is all your hard work. You deserve every bit of the appreciation you get."

"Just be with me like this always Piya. Then I can scale all heights with ease."

"Oh Abir....what do I do without you?! Even if I want to, I can never stay away from you." Piya hugged Abir tightly, and a drop of a tear rolled down her cheeks. She wondered which hidden hurt suddenly spurred this tear. Then she realized, that it was not the hurt but the love she felt for him that so whelmed her with a rush of joy that her words could not express the depth of that love and hence, it took the form of a tear to escape her heart.

Abir did not want to let Piya go but he was the more mature among the two, so he ultimately had to. He was sensible and sensitive but not sentimental. He pampered Piya to the core but propelled her to do her best at the same time.

"Come on now Piya, get packing fast. The rate at which you are packing, it seems you are going to spend all night doing this."

"No no I am done. I am anyway sleepy. Have to catch the early morning flight tomorrow." saying this Piya got up and bade goodnight to Abir. He lazily sauntered behind her wondering how on earth would he survive so many days without his Piya.

Next day in the wee hours of the morning Abir drove Piya to the airport. As Piya went inside, he drove away with clouds of thoughts running through his mind.

Piya landed at Bombay exactly at 8.50 AM. The conference was to be held in the famous Y2K hotel at Bandra Kurla Complex, barely a fifteen minutes drive from the domestic airport. The morning traffic delayed her by a few minutes. She made her way through to the reception fifteen past nine. While getting herself registered, she felt that she saw him.

She quickly completed the formalities without wasting much time as the program was expected to begin sharp at half past nine.

The banquet was huge. Since she was late, she got a seat towards the rear exit of the banquet.

She could not concentrate on the conference much. Her eyes wandered looking for the figure she vaguely thought resembled him.

Just five minutes before the recess, she spotted him again. He was busy checking his mobile recklessly. She decided to wait till the recess to greet him. But all this while, she wondered, how in these years he had changed so much.

In the next five minutes she tried making up for the lost interest by concentrating hard on the conference. But in a blink the session broke. Before she could collect her belongings and move out of the row to approach him, he was gone again.

She lazily dragged herself to the dining hall reminiscing about her past. She nibbled on a sandwich while checking on the points that she would be delivering in the post lunch session as one of the speakers. All along, her mind trailing the path leading to Joy.

The session started on a very good note. Dignitaries listened to her with apt attention when she spotted him again. He was nervously typing on his smartphone. She found it pretty awkward. She got distracted for a split second but gathered herself up and continued with élan.

After her presentation, a few others followed, after which, the session broke for tea. That is when she saw him standing at the smoking bay facing the outer railing of the balcony. She slowly walked up to him planning to surprise him. Instead, she was in for a rude shock.

She overheard him speak on his phone, "What nonsense are you speaking? You know the typical storage time is less than twelve hours for a liver. How can you transport it to such a place?" After a brief pause, he continued, "Ok. Carry on. The money must be deposited in my account in not more than twelve hours."

Piya thought there is a missing link to what he said. She could not get to think what he was upto. In the meantime, he turned around to see Piya standing right behind him. He broke into a cold sweat and Piya sensed something. She had expected him to be happy on seeing her. But no, he was not.

He finally broke the silence awkwardly mumbling, "Hi Piya, what a surprise! How have you been?"

"I am happy Joy. What about you?" Piya questioned staring straight into his eyes.

Joy looked stirred. He simply managed to say, "Are you upset that I did not return your call?"

"Do you really bother Joy?" was Piya's curt reply.

Joy was silent for a while.

"You spoke well Piya. So what is happening with you these days?"

"Can we meet over a cup of coffee and chat Joy?"

"Umm well no I am sort of pre-occupied."

Piya immediately felt a sting in her heart. Why did she have to invite him for coffee, she repented. Just then her phone buzzed. Piya excused herself to take the call.

Piya was not excited to see Abir's number flashing on her phone. Very casually she answered the call.

"Did I not tell you Piya you are my lucky charm?"

"Why what happened?"

"I am seeing you tomorrow evening in Bombay to give you the details. Wait for my call." Abir hung up.

Piya was taken aback for a split second. She could not reason why. She loved Abir and enjoyed his company. Then what is bothering her? Why is she not excited to know what is on Abir's mind. When her own mental predicament kept bugging her, she decided to just leave it at that and wait till the next day.

The next day at the conference was uneventful for Piya. Joy kept on avoiding eye contact with her. She too, ashamed of the previous day's rendezvous with him, maintained a distance. But nevertheless, she wondered how Joy had changed over these years. Not only in his demeanour, but in his physical appearance as well. He was no more the childish young brat who loved food, hated studies and was a cute little pest. He had now grown into a handsome young man. The curls falling on his forehead had transformed into a receding hairline and his dimples were tauter now. His complexion had slightly tanned but what remained the same was the small black mole on the right side of his chin.

In the evening, Piya received Abir at the airport and the first thing she said even before greeting him was "Tell me what you made me wait for since yesterday."

Abir hugged her and whispered in her ears, "Congratulations. You are now the wife of Senior Reporter, Special Crime Branch, India Times."

Piya was ecstatic. She felt so proud of Abir's achievement that she could barely mumble a congratulation to him. Rather she just clung to Abir like a happy child who clings to the father after a much awaited merry-go-round ride.

Abir continued, "I thought of flying to Bombay so that I could break the news to you personally and at the same time, we both could finalize a house together before we shift to Bombay bag and baggage once you return home."

Piya could never disagree with Abir, such was his reasoning always. Rather, all his plans were such that these were carved out especially keeping her wish in mind.

For the next couple of days, while Piya attended the conference till evening, Abir shortlisted the homes and then they went together in the late evenings to see the houses. A day before they were slotted to return, they finalized a beautiful two bedroom furnished apartment with a view of the creek in the western suburban locality called Borivali. That was the same creek where she had first gone out with Joy. But now, Piya was a changed woman. The creek did not even remind her of her rendezvous with Joy though it was certainly a happy memory.

CHAPTER 17

Abir and Piya had settled in their new pad which they not only called home, but came to feel so. Their flat at Kolkata remained as it is and here they bought everything new for their rented apartment. Piya had applied to SSKM Hospital from where she had done her internship and had got through. She was now a full time practitioner there. Abir was well settled in his new role and was constantly looking for some meaty stuff for his section. Shortly after, Abir was no ordinary name in the journalism business and thanks to his profession, he enjoyed unfettered access to corridors of power.

Abir and Piya enjoyed a new life, a new role and a home away from home. They would occasionally go partying at night or just stroll over to the creek and enjoy the cool breeze blowing through their faces. They would sometimes go out for dinner to posh restaurants or at times simply to 'khau galli' which was the famous place for street food joints.

Piya often observed that the best part of being married to Abir was that she never got bored of life. She was happy and peaceful. They never fought over frivolous matters. Infact the only time they fought was when she had sent a text message from her phone to Abir saying *"luv u"*. Abir responded curtly, *"I do not like it when people write about 'love' as 'luv'. To me it demeans love. If now you cannot spare your time to write 1 alphabet more, do you really think you will have enough time for me all your life?"* Piya felt bad at his reply. But then she realized she loved him for what he is. He stands up for what he means. His face reflects what his heart feels. Piya loved this Abir and everything about him.

All they craved was each other's company. What made their relationship special was that they both resonated each other's feelings. Piya thought about that and felt lucky. She thought atleast she was not stuck in a loveless marriage and felt Abir was not only her life partner, but her soul mate.

Soon after, Piya, being a doctor, realized that happiness was getting the better of her health and that, if she did not steer her life in the right direction, she might hit the hidden icebergs of diseases like diabetes, obesity, etc. So she got into a habit of taking early morning walks to the creek every day. Abir usually returned very late from work as the nature of his work demanded it. So it became impossible for him to accompany Piya for her morning walks. Bombay was a pleasant place to live in. Though the winter mornings were dark in Bombay, during the remaining nine months, the sky was full of light quite early and by eight in the morning, the sun shone bright as noon.

Piya dismissed her alarm sharp at 5.30 AM daily and after getting fresh, she was out latest by six. The creek was just round the corner from their apartment and so, she reached in no time. She walked for about forty five minutes, then did free hand exercise for about half an hour and returned home by half past seven.

While at the creek, exercising or walking, everyday, she met an old man. He looked elegantly handsome even at this age. He appeared to be in his mid sixties. He had a broad but steep nose and a thick mop of curly hair, absolutely milk white in colour and cropped short. He wore a beard, trimmed to perfection, camouflaging a soft jawline. He had deep, sensitive eyes and an enigmatic smile. Short eyebrows, cringed and pursed lips were his trademark features. He came to walk his dog and appeared to be a very loving and caring person albeit caged within his own solitude.

The gregarious girl that she was, who ran up to almost every person who appeared to be nice and eventually appealed to her heart, she one day, just wandered over to him. Something about him, drew her. The first line that Piya spoke was not to him though. She simply snuggled the dog, and tenderly asked, "Hello sweet thing! What do I call you as?"

That is when she heard him speak. His voice was so soft that when he spoke, it felt like a ball of cotton thrown at one's ears. He just mumbled, "Scamper."

No greetings, no pleasantries exchanged. Just a simple one word answer. Piya's spirit sagged slightly. But the unrelenting woman that she was with such an indomitable spirit that she took that one word as an opportunity to start a conversation with the old man.

"Oh! Nice name. Suits this little pet."

"Thank you." Another curt reply followed.

The more the old man avoided her, the more resolute she grew in her pursuit. She was so adroit at handling problems that she at times casually wondered that where did her skill vanish when she was pursuing Joy!

Piya this time, in expectation of getting an upper hand, held out her hand for a handshake. "Hi, I am Piya. I stay just around the corner. And you sir?"

"Das. Kedar Das." Still a James Bond style curt reply. But hearing his name, Piya jumped with joy! Without waiting to let him continue, she shrieked with delight, "Wow! You too are a Bengali?"

"No. I am an Indian. I belong to the province of Maharashtra." He smiled back as he replied.

Piya was mighty impressed at this. Just to keep the conversation alive, she said, "Hmm....but why do you say so? Are not those who belong to the province of Maharashtra, called Maharashtrians?"

"They are. But I prefer it this way. It is a long story." Saying this with yet another smile, he started walking away as Scamper scampered ahead.

Piya called behind, "Maybe some other day..." Her voice trailed off as she felt he did not even listen to her.

Piya went on with her usual routine. That day, while at the hospital, during lunch, she was just surfing the internet while munching on a veg grilled sandwich when she suddenly thought of checking up whether Kedar Das was on any social media. She simply googled Kedar Das and lo and behold, he was not only on social media, but he was on Wikipedia, which meant he was an important personality!

She read through his profile with the urgency with which a student studies on the last night before the exam. She was surprised to find out that he was a retired University Reader in Experimental Psychology at Department of Experimental Psychology, Medical Sciences Division at University of Oxford. He did his PhD from the very same University and had spent most of his life in the

United Kingdom. Dr. Das had published extensively on Experimental Psychology and post retirement, was a full time high level nonfiction writer, which included his essays, and articles, besides writing in medical journals related to Experimental Psychology.

Piya could not believe she spoke to a man of his stature. She was now determined to speak to him again. She found interacting with such people very intellectually stimulating. She waited for the next day's morning walk session like never before.

Next morning, Piya was awake even before it was half past five. She was already ready to go out when a sleepy Abir murmured, "What is motivating you so much darling that you are not even waiting for your alarm clock to buzz?"

"I will tell you once I am back!" Was Piya's curt reply albeit with a twinkle in her eyes, which was enough to make Abir's day!

He turned around for a second round of sleep while Piya jogged out and down the staircase, forming dialogues in her head, in her determination to befriend him.

Piya knew he would first walk his dog along the jogger's track running parallel to the creek and then sit on one of those benches dotting the boundary wall of lawn where she exercised. So she deliberately walked in tandem with Dr. Das in order to open casual conversation with the scholar.

He stopped at the entrance of the lawn and looked at her. In the eye. Piya was flabbergasted. She did not know what to do when his question nailed her. "What?" He simply asked. Piya gulped down her saliva in a vague notion of quenching her thirst, the sense of which her parched throat exuded.

He repeated, "I thought you wanted to say something?" Piya still could not move. He was quite straightforward, "Well if you do not want to then fine. I am sorry." Saying this, he started moving ahead, leaving Piya transfixed in her place.

She was brought back to her senses by a wailing child who had fallen off the aisle.

She first ran towards the child and seeing his mother pick him up, she strode towards where she expected Dr. Das to be seated, watching Scamper scamper through the lawn.

The moment she reached the lawn, she spotted him seated at the usual place and strode over to him so that she could answer him. But even before she could say sorry for not responding to his questions earlier, he spoke with a smile, "I see that you wanted to be here but you first headed to pick up the child. Good. It is good to see people with a heart these days."

This time Piya responded with a smile, "I do not know whether I am drawn to kids because of my heart or because of the fact that I am a paediatrician. But all

I know is that the moment I see a child in distress, my heart bleeds."

"Well! There you go! So you know you have a good heart and not that of a thorough professional."

"You identify people well, do you not?" This time it was Piya's turn to guess.

"Yes. That is partially because of my strong senses and partially because of my education. And before you ask, let me tell you, I deal with....."

"....Experimental Psychology" Piya stopped him midway to complete his sentence.

His brows cringed, "So you have researched well about me." He said half smiling.

Piya chuckled and narrated to him how she got to his bio. Dr. Das was amused at this. He never found somebody who would go to this extent to make her voice heard to someone she barely knows.

Seeing his expression, when Piya was quite sure that he would not retort, she put forth her hand sheepishly, "So, sir, friends?"

He dismissed her with a wave of his hand and said, "Aah! You want to be friends with someone whom you address as Sir?"

Piya was baffled. She did not know how to handle Dr. Das. He surprised Piya at every step. Piya did not know what to make of that statement when he responded, "I can be friends with you if you call me Kedar."

"You mind being friends if I call you KD instead??" Pat came Piya's reply, who was visibly uncomfortable addressing a revered person of her father's age by his first name.

"I do not mind. If you want me to be KD instead of Kedar, so be it. But buddy, give me one reason why you wanted to be friends with a withered old man like me?"

"Friendship pervades one's soul. It cannot be bound by reasons." Was Piya's smart response that ignited another true blue friendship, which was never to be justified or questioned; a relation that was beyond age, gender, caste, creed, beliefs and faiths. A friendship, which was never to be measured in time. A relation that was beyond the passage of time.

Before KD could say another word, Piya jumped up, "Oh God I am late! I got to be going KD. I will see you tomorrow again. Same time."

KD simply waved at her and she was gone in a flash.

Back home, Piya was all ecstatic about her new friend and Abir listened to her endless animated chatter enthusiastically.

There was nothing in Piya's life that would put a crease on her forehead until the day she met Lalu.

CHAPTER 18

Piya was as usual busy visiting the children's ward when the ward boys and nurses wheeled a child in critical condition to the ward. The child was writhing in pain. Though her profession demanded that she does not get emotional about any patient, but this child's suffering somehow melted her. She sprung to action and after giving him a temporary sedative to calm him down, she advised a couple of tests including an Ultra Sono Graphy (USG) of the complete abdomen.

Once the child lay to rest, the father of the child, who identified himself as Lalchand Hirani aka Lalu, started crying with his hands folded with his raised palms touching each other in a 'namaste' in front of his chest, "Madam, please save my child. I am a poor man working as a ward boy in the Bombay Medical School and Nursing Home. My son, Chhotu complained of pain on the right side of his abdomen and so I rushed him there immediately. After a week, his pain became unbearable and I was told it was just few hours for him to succumb to his pain. I immediately thought of shifting him here because he was almost on the verge of collapsing and needed further treatment which would be expensive at the nursing home I work for."

Piya became stiff at the mention of Bombay Medical School and Nursing Home. She was even more shaken knowing that the child was shifted out of the hospital in that critical condition for lack of funds. Especially when the boy's father was an employee there. Piya sighed. She thought to herself, '*Possibly Joy did not know about this incident. He cannot change so much. Had he known, he would have treated the child for free.*'

Nevertheless, she went on with her patients while waiting patiently for the USG report to come.

Finally, in the afternoon, the USG report reached her desk. The report left her aghast. It showed, the boy was functioning with only one kidney and was in a critical stage.

Piya questioned Lalu persistently to unravel the obscurity of Chhotu's health. When Lalu's answers could not satisfy her fully, she ran to Chhotu's bedside. She flung the sheet covering the sleeping child and pushed up his shirt to reveal his torso. Her brows cringed, her teeth gritted. She touched the scar on the child's right abdomen lightly with her fingers. She immediately got up, covered him and left the room. Lalu followed her as if he was hypnotized.

Piya dashed at her chamber straight and picked up the desk phone. Even after so many years and after so many unpleasant events, she remembered Joy's mobile number by heart. She frantically dialed his number. No answer. She dialed again. Still no answer. She went crazy. She dug into her handbag now and reached for her mobile, dialing his number frantically. This time Joy picked up her call. Just as she was about to speak, he said, "Piya, next time you call me, please make sure to call at the hospital number so that my secretary can screen through the call and pass it on to me only if it is extremely urgent and important." Piya was taken aback. But Joy's words did not deter her to say what she wanted to. "Joy what is the matter with Chhotu?"

Joy sounded irritated. "What? Who Chhotu? Piya have you called me to……"

Piya cut him off midway. "Joy Chhotu is the son of Lalchand Hirani, your ward boy."

The mention of Lalu rang a bell. "What is with him? Pass him on the phone." Joy felt queasy.

Piya was hell-bent on finding out the details now. "Joy you will have to speak to me now. Chhotu was admitted to your nursing home and his pain intensified for which Lalu brought him here. And now I found out that one of his kidneys are gone! What is the matter?"

"What? Brought him here means? Are you still in Bombay? When did you shift here?" Joy tried deviating the topic.

"Do not play smart with me Joy. Tell me all that happened with Chhotu at your nursing home." Piya retorted.

This time, Joy chose offence over defense to tackle her. "Who do you think you are talking to Piya? You think just because you studied in the same class with me, you can say anything and everything to me? Do you even understand whom you are talking to? You are questioning the CEO of Bombay Medical School and Nursing Home about a ward boy's son? Get a life Piya. And do not bother to disturb me ever again." He hung up after shouting his temper off.

Piya was stunned. The precarious claims that joy made surprised her. But she gained back her composure and became more resolute in solving the mystery of the missing kidney.

She then decided to take help of Lalu to put together the pieces of the puzzle. That night, when she opened the door to Abir, he read something strange in her facial expression. He simply hugged her and said, "Look Piya, I cannot make poetries like your favourite poets, but that does not mean I do not love you with all that I have. So tell me what is bothering you; I cannot bear seeing a frown on your face."

Piya rested her head onto his chest and just sighed. He knew something grave was bothering her. He decided to get fresh and sit with her in a relaxed mood.

Piya was ready with dinner when he came out of the shower. They ate in silence. Abir decided to delve into Piya's silence. So he made coffee and sat by the window with Piya. The window overlooked the creek. They both held their cups in their hands and had the other hand entangled in each other's. They did not stare at each other, but together they stared at the creek. Piya rested her head on his shoulder.

Abir broke the silence. "What is the matter Piya? Do I not deserve to know what is playing on your mind?"

Abir's words echoed back, having hit the stony wall created by Piya's silence hard.

Piya sighed again. Abir decided to give Piya the space she demanded, knowing full well he is the first person she will open up to, when the time was right.

Next morning, Piya was in no mood to go for her walk. However, she decided not to skip walking for she knew if she missed walking due to something that bothered her, it would only add to the stress rather than reducing it. Plus, she felt that probably breathing in the fresh air and chatting with her buddy will only free her of her stress.

So off she went for her morning walk.

There, KD awaited her. The moment he saw her walking in to the park, he could feel that the natural glitter in Piya's eyes was missing. Being the kind of a person who could read people's minds, Dr. Das could understand immediately that something bothered Piya. It was not very long that Piya and KD now knew each other. Yet, they felt a kinship towards each other that ran deeper than words could find way. So armouring his authority with that kinship, Dr. Das went two steps ahead towards her and authoritatively asked, "Oh! Who has been naughty enough to put a crease on my little buddy's forehead?" Dr. Das was as much caring as little he appeared. But every pore in his body oozed tender care. Not towards anyone in particular, but towards all that came along his way. He could not open up to people easily but once he did, he would be the best friend a person can get. Such was his nature.

But Piya was in no mood to answer such saccharine coated, overtly sentimental fairy tale lines. She snapped, "KD something is genuinely bothering me and the matter is incomprehensibly serious."

KD was taken aback for a while. But he knew something must be really bothering Piya for her to react like that. He wanted to comfort her but did not know how unless he knew of the whole stuff. And Piya would not give out the details to anyone. Not even to Abir, leave alone anyone else.

KD did not pursue the matter and just let Piya be, saying only - "This too shall pass Piya". That was a motivation strong enough for Piya to keep going. Her determination steely enough to solve all mysteries.

She felt she was rude to KD by answering him back like that. She felt repentant. So in order to make things good, she started debating on the world famous topic of 'women are at par with men on all grounds' hoping to elicit some clue about digging into men's mind. She knew KD was an experimental psychologist and would speak out of his huge experience and knowledge, which might give her some headway in solving the mystery of the missing kidney. They usually discussed on diverse topics ranging from astronomical developments to new movie releases. So KD did not even realize why Piya picked this topic suddenly. He, enamoured, replied, "I do not understand why is our generation so busy trying to prove what women can do at par with men. In the process, they do not realize that they are losing their uniqueness and in the process, they are forgetting that they are capable to do much beyond men's capability."

That answer, though did not satiate Piya's need to delve into men's or specifically so Joy's mind, but was enough to satiate her hunger for inspiration. She proceeded home feeling a lot lighter than her morning mood made her feel.

Once home from her morning walk, she got ready, scribbled a note for Abir, apologizing for her last night's erratic behaviour, put it under his bowl of cereals and hurried for her hospital while he was fast asleep. This was a habit they had inculcated as their own. That was a very private part of their relationship that they fiercely guarded. Very often, they resorted to handwritten notes like this. And that only brought them closer.

The moment she was at her desk, she called Lalu. Lalu was sleeping at the waiting area of the hospital. He had stayed put at the hospital for Chhotu. Lalu came rushing to her cabin on getting her call, worried of his son's health.

"Listen Lalu. Chhotu will be completely alright in a month's rest. He will have to be completely bed-ridden for this one month. But I can smell some foul play in all this. You will have to help me nab those who played with your son's life."

Lalu looked shocked and at the same time confused. He could not fathom why someone would play with his son's life. He did not understand what could little Chhotu's life mean to someone. But he trusted Piya. Because, she saved his son.

When Lalu nodded his approval, Piya detailed him with the plan on how to go about it. She knew Joy in and out. She thought it will not be difficult to find out his whereabouts.

They were now a team. A team against evil.

After her conversation with Lalu, she felt slightly relaxed and decided to call Abir. Abir said he would be home early, thinking Piya needed his company even more now.

Lalu went back to the nursing home where he worked to meet Joy when Joy confronted him. "What happened to your son?" He asked, slightly worried.

"Sir, I am a poor man and could not afford my son's treatment here when his pain aggravated. So I shifted him to the government hospital." He stopped to breathe.

"But a female doctor from the government hospital called me asking about your son. Did she tell you anything?"

"Sir you cannot really compare those government hospitals with nursing homes like yours and certainly cannot compare those government hospital doctors with foreign return doctors like you. Probably she did not understand what the matter with my Chhotu is so she possibly must have called you. As it is I also heard that she was your classmate so maybe she thought she can seek your guidance in this matter. But do not worry sir, she will not bother you again as I told her I work for you and that my sir remains very busy to look into such small cases." Lalu said casually.

Joy calmed down with Lalu's response wondering what a stupid man Lalu was and walked away without realizing, every word that Lalu said was totally orchestrated.

In the evening, once they both were home, Abir felt relaxed seeing Piya calm and composed. That night, they had ordered food from their favourite joint and the food was already delivered home. He planned on surprising her with some romantic gesture. So he rushed Piya to get fresh and knowing that she will not be out before half an hour, he laid the table for dinner, lit with scented candles and dimmed the lights of the living cum dining room. Then he placed a plate full of her favourite dark chocolates right in the middle of the table and switched on a DVD that Piya had compiled for him. The room was soon filled with soft instrumentals by Kenny G, Yehudi Menuhin, Mozart and Bach.

Abir suddenly realized Piya's phone buzz. He picked it up and saw the name 'Lalu (Joy)' flashing. He was intrigued. *Who could be Lalu and how was he connected with Joy? Could this call be related to the reason of Piya's discomfort for the last two days?* He answered the call to answer the questions running through his mind.

Even before he could say 'hello', Lalu whooped, "Madam, I have done as you said. Joy sir is not suspecting me in anything. I told him my son is getting better and that is what matters to me. I join office again tomorrow. I will keep you posted on the developments. Hello, madam, are you listening?"

This time, Abir spoke. "This is your madam's husband on the line Lalu. She is very upset. Tell me what the matter is."

Lalu fumbled. Piya had warned him to keep this a secret. "Sir, please forgive me. Madam asked me to keep it a secret and I cannot share it with anybody."

Abir was desperate. "Lalu I work as a Senior Reporter in Special Crime Branch of India Times. I promise to help you. Do not be scared of me. Your madam probably does not want me to know as she does not want me to be bothered by anything. But I can surely help in this regard."

Lalu sensed Abir was not wrong. He decided to let him know the details but was scared as well. He finally mustered up courage and said, "Sir, even I want to help madam because she has saved my son's life. But promise me you will not tell her that I gave you out the secret."

Abir swore by Piya that he will not reveal anything unless the case was resolved and Lalu told him all about his son, about the missing kidney and about their plan. Now the team comprised three of them - Piya, Lalu and Abir.

Piya came out of the shower and the scene enchanted her to the point of tears. She felt overwhelmed at the intensity with which Abir tried to make her feel better.

Abir came forward, wrapped his slender arm around her and with the free hand, wiped off her tears and said, "Do not worry sweetheart. I will free you of all your worries." Then he kissed her eyelids gently whispering, "Come darling, this moment awaits our togetherness."

Piya, momentarily, forgot all about Joy. Only peace prevailed in their abode.

CHAPTER 19

Piya kept in regular touch with Lalu. A couple of months had passed and Piya's doubt about Joy was gradually being shaped into a belief by small snippets of news that Lalu passed on to her. He had started giving her printouts of letters or emails that he sent and had started recording his voice calls, though one sided, on his own mobile phone, that Piya had bought for him. Piya kept a record of every detail that she got from Lalu. What she was oblivious to was that Abir stood rock solid behind her and kept a copy of exactly the same documents too. What Abir did with all that, nobody knew. But Piya was keeping all those records to substantiate proof good enough against Joy to get him nabbed when the time came.

In the meantime, she continued on her morning walks, went to the hospital regularly, went out with Abir, and maintained normalcy in life.

One fine morning, as she walked side by side her friend KD in the jogging track, he declared he was leaving. She was aghast!

"What are you saying KD? Who will I chat with now going forward on my morning walks?"

"Little Lady, life goes on and you go with the flow. Destiny is the river and time is the boat. You flow with time but follow the tide of the water, which is exactly what is written in your destiny."

"Yeah but can you please explain what makes you take this sudden decision?" Piya almost wailed like a child.

"My son is shifting to Pennsylvania to teach at the Pennsylvania Institute of Art and Design. I am shifting with him. I do not want him to be alone till the time he gets married as he anyway craves for his mother. I do not want him to crave for me now. Shall visit India once in a year though."

Tears welled up in Piya's eyes. She had become great friends with KD in this wee time. She felt hurt to let him go. But had to. She simply looked at him and said, "Will you stay in touch?"

KD too felt a lump in his throat. He had started liking Piya as his own daughter. He promised to write to her often.

Piya felt stressed. Reason one being the mystery of the missing kidney and reason two being KD leaving. She wanted to set her life free, free of all worries, but it seemed to get entangled in all that she did not want. So to relieve her stress, she invited KD over for dinner to her place over the weekend. KD barely had a fortnight to go and hence, hesitated. But Piya was stubborn.

"Come on! I cannot let you go without getting you introduced to Abir. You are now my best friend, and Abir knows all my friends. So how is it possible that he will never see you?" She argued.

Piya's relentless insistence made him agree. It was decided that KD will come over to Piya's house on the coming Saturday for dinner.

Back home, Piya was all excited. She had momentarily forgotten about the missing kidney. Or so it appeared from her happiness emanating self. Abir was happy to see Piya so happy after a very long time. And when Abir sat down to plan out the evening with Piya, she was ecstatic.

It was decided that Piya will not spend too much time cooking but make her signature dishes that she was sure KD would love to have. Then they decided on a special gift for KD that they would give to him as a parting gift.

On the designated night, KD arrived wearing a black shirt and blue jeans. Piya and Abir offered him a warm welcome. After the regular pleasantries were exchanged, and after the welcome drinks were served, they sat down to chat. Abir and Piya noted down his email address and KD too did.

The dinner was over soon with KD appreciating the brilliance of Piya's culinary skills. He was awed that Piya could manage home and kitchen so well besides managing her patients at once.

Abir beamed with pride at this. He always knew that he had married the best girl he deserved. Today, with a stranger appreciating her so much, he swelled with pride more.

After dessert was served, they sat together for a long chat and clicked photographs together; KD and Piya shared with Abir how they had met. Abir politely listened to the whole story again though Piya had already told him the entire story over and over again. Such was Abir's Piya. Unless and until she told Abir everything, multiple number of times, she could not rest. And Abir enjoyed this.

Then came the parting time. Abir and Piya gave him a gift wrapped box with a bon voyage card attached to its top. KD was pleasantly surprised and asked Piya what was in it. She said with a smile, "It is a mini refractor telescope used for stargazing."

"Piya, you remembered? Aah! I cannot believe that you remembered." KD enthused.

"KD, I pay apt attention to whatever you say. How could I have not remembered?" Piya chirped happily and then went on to tell Abir the story of how she decided on a telescope as a farewell gift for KD.

"You know Abir, KD loved stargazing as a kid. His father would stand next to him in the nights and trace the Milky Way with him on clear skies. He used to love being so close to his father. Now that his father himself has become a star according to him, he feels closer to him through astronomy. Since his childhood he loved stargazing so much that when he grew up, even as concrete high rises took over the clear space, he bought books on astronomy to keep himself updated.

So KD, please gaze at those stars at night and remember us. Remember that we too are gazing at the same stars." Saying this Piya choked on her emotions.

KD too felt overwhelmingly emotional, yet, he took out a small package wrapped carefully with a silver coloured paper, handed it over to Piya, kissed on her forehead, and said, "Piya, this contains an hourglass. I got it for you thinking of the good times we shared together. But this is also to remind you that time passes by in a blink. So in life, always remember, what you do, probably nobody will notice it immediately, but beyond the passage of time, it will be etched forever in your heart. So consciously, never do any wrong. I hope you remember me always, with these last parting words of mine."

Thus a beautiful page turned over in Piya's life.

From morning walk friends, she and KD became mail friends. They continued writing to each other often.

KD would often go for a walk across the road trail along the Grand Canyon of Pennsylvania and come back and write about his experiences to Piya. He would spot new flowers and describe their beauty to her. He would see animals like a raccoon, birds like the great blue heron and write back to Piya about all that. He would write to her how he learned to prepare a Spanish Omelette and she would ask him for the recipe. She would write to him about how she loved white orchids. He would write back saying he will remember her when he saw white orchids. She would say it was windy and chilly today, he would reply saying it snowed heavily. The time difference between the two places where Piya and KD resided was nine and a half hours. When KD would have his morning tea at seven thirty, Piya would have hers in the evening at five, while chatting together online. And thus, life went on and on for them, exchanging emails as if they had a portion of each other in their daily lives; as if they never parted.

Piya used to write regularly to KD. But that did not mean that she ignored the main heart thumping cause that bewildered her. She was as happy to suddenly have an email friend as she was agonized to be unable to sort out the mystery of the missing kidney.

Abir all along kept mum. He did not disclose to Piya that he was doing all that was in his power to help Piya out of her perplexity.

He thought Piya would not like it if he stepped in to help her. Probably, her independent self will hurt her ego. But what he did not understand was that it would probably have helped Piya.

Several months had passed since Piya had treated Chhotu, Lalu's son and now she was getting impatient to resolve the case. But she had a lot of work left to put the puzzle in place. She had no other way but to wait for some solid proof that would nail the culprit.

CHAPTER 20

Abir returned home at three in the night, opened the front door and hung the keys on the key holder kept on the mantel. He took a quick shower, got into comfortable night wear and sneaked into the bed next to Piya, careful not to wake up his sleeping beauty.

But Piya, knew the touch of his skin, she knew his fragrance. Even in deep sleep, she could feel him. Just as Abir lay on his back, Piya turned to face him and smiled, "What time is it Abir?" He was apologetic, "Did I wake you up sweetheart? It is half past three now."

Piya smiled, "How do you expect me to sleep when you are not there next to me? I was only reading and do not know when I slipped into a deep slumber. But how come you are so late tonight?"

He propped himself up on one elbow to face her, "Piya there is something I wish to share with you. If you are sleepy we can talk tomorrow."

Piya smiled, "If your heart wishes to share something with mine, how do you expect mine not to care? Tell me darling, I am all ears."

Piya looked beautiful in this moonlit room. Especially when she spoke like this. Abir's heart skipped a beat. He did not want to ruin this moment. But he wanted Piya to be free of all her worries.

"Brace yourself Piya. I have some bad news."

Piya's brows cringed. "Tell me Abir. I am strong enough to withstand anything unfavourable as long as you are with me."

"It is estimated that almost half the number of organs that are transplanted are from illegal human trafficking. A heinous racket has been busted in relation to organ trade. And Joy, has been convicted as the main brain behind the same in this city. He has been acquitted of kidnapping and killing minors for organ trade. He infact not only stopped at that, he also targeted the poverty ravaged slums of Bombay and in lieu of hefty sums and an assurance of a lifetime free treatment, he made the poor men sell off one or more of their organs. He has reduced human life to its flesh value. It is such a gruesome crime that this has shocked even the hard-bitten cops." Abir stopped to breathe.

Piya was too shocked to even ask him how did he know all these. She fought hard to believe what she had just heard.

Abir held her to make her feel better. But she was beyond the stage of feeling now. She did not know what to do or say. She was shocked beyond repair.

Abir thought of calming her down by giving her out the details. He told her how he got in touch with Lalu and apologized for not revealing to her earlier that he was working on this as he wanted to respect Piya's decision of not telling him. Then he very carefully detailed to her the way he unraveled the mystery. "You know Piya, when Lalu told me that he doubted Joy was into organ trade by his telephonic conversations and the documents that he made Lalu handle, I planned to nail him right then. I requested Lalu to hand me over all the copies of his mails and letters, including his itemized phone bills. I took the audio files of his telephonic recordings too. Precisely, whichever document Lalu handed over to you, he gave me too. I maintained a file and when I was convinced enough, I immediately requested for a private audience with Mr. Mike Vaz, the Commissioner of Police and discussed this matter directly with him. I handed over to him copies of all his emails, letters, and even voice recordings that Lalu gave me. Mr. Vaz kept everything under wraps but kept on investigating the matter, including getting his phone tapped, until one agent through whom Joy used to export the organs was arrested. He broke down under Police investigation and named the who's who of the racket. That is how our dear friend got arrested."

Piya simply said, "Now I know what he was talking about on phone when I saw him at the medical conference and why his face suddenly turned bloodless seeing me. Which also means, he had got one of Chhotu's kidneys removed to sell it off when the poor boy went to him for treatment!"

She suddenly turned emotional. It was possibly the outcome of a sense of victory over evil, blended with her guilt of not identifying the kind of person that Joy was. Tears streamed down her eyes flowing onto her cheeks. Abir held her pacifying her to the best of his ability. And in no time it was time for the newspaper to arrive.

Piya hurried to get the newspaper and opened it to find the headline stare back at her - "Illegal organ trafficking trade exposed", reports Abir Ray, Senior Reporter, Crime Branch.

She gulped down the article in no time. She looked at Abir and said, "I wish to see him in Jail. Please arrange for the visit." Piya sounded so resolute that Abir did not even think of dissuading her. Rather, accompanied her lest she gets into some sort of a trouble.

That morning, as Piya and Joy stood face to face, Abir told Piya he would be waiting for her outside and left them to themselves.

For few seconds, Piya simply stood staring at his face. Joy broke the silence, "Piya, I...." Piya's raised hand had stopped him from speaking further.

"Don't you dare speak Joy. You have spoken enough. I, infact am marveled at how delicately and intricately you have entwined the lies, one by one, just for the sake of riches and power. Why Joy? What did you not have? You had everything to make yourself happy. Then why Joy?" This time Piya's sobs stopped her midway.

Joy tried pacifying her, "Do not cry for me Piya. I have got what I deserved. And I do not have any repentance for that. Whatever be my fate now, I will accept it with open arms."

Piya simply said, "You have woven such a web of lies that it is hard to see how you can extricate yourself now. But if you ever manage to get out of here freely again Joy, please remember always to raise your standard of life, not your standard of living."

Saying this, Piya turned around to leave. "I know why you are crying Piya." Joy's voice stopped her raised step.

Piya stood still; she turned around to face Joy but did not speak a word.

"Yes Piya. I know how much you still love me. But I have lost all that I had. The riches, power, and of course, your love."

Piya was stunned. "You knew?" she just managed to mumble.

"Yes. I knew it. You never said so but you certainly made me realize how much you love me. Though I never believed you could love a boy like me. I just somehow knew. Maybe because I too loved you truly."

"Joy, please do not even talk about love. It does not suit you. The fact is, I felt love for you, the kind of love that I, as an adolescent, read about in books. As and when I grew up, I realized it was not what is actually called love. Because love does not come alone. It needs to be supplemented with reverence, care and trust. And I never felt reverence for you. Now I definitely do not trust you. Yes I always cared for you but not anymore. You have destined your own ruin. Now you cool your heels here. My life outside awaits me."

Just as she turned, she saw Abir staring at her flashing his signature smile. "This, is only the beginning darling."

He held Piya by her shoulders and walked her away from Joy, towards a life full of joy.

CHAPTER 21

Piya was being wheeled into the operation theatre as Abir looked on tense. She was unconscious. Prof. Roy and Mrs. Roy looked on anxiously. Mrs. Ray's lips murmured in a silent prayer though not even a single word of it could be heard. Mr. Ray was as always unfazed by any anxiety and looked calm. But that did not quite mean that he was not tensed.

The environment was as it is nervy. The red light outside the operation theatre, indicating an ongoing surgery, made it even queasier. Nobody spoke.

It was a bright day outside with clear blue sky. Winter had bid goodbye but still there was a chill in the air. Birds chirped happily indicating spring. It was March 2nd. It was exactly five years back that on this day, Abir and Piya had tied the knot. But this year, there was no celebration. This year, the lips of their well wishers were adorned not with wishes for them, but with prayers for Piya.

Abir consciously kept on reminiscing about their wedding day and the last couple of year's celebration. What a grand celebration the first year after wedding was! Afterall it was the first year anniversary celebration. They both did not merely celebrate their union. Rather, they celebrated their love. In the second year they went on a mini honeymoon again. Some tourists there asked them if they were newly married though they had spent two years together. How happy they had looked together. But even these lovely thoughts could not keep Abir free of worry. It seemed he was dying thousand deaths in these moments that swept away.

After about an hour, the light turned green. They all eagerly moved ahead. Abir almost sprinted to be there first. And out came the doctor with a mini replica of Piya in her arms. Abir was transfixed in his position. The cute little thing cradled in the doctor's arm was just so perfect! And what made it even more desirable for Abir was that it resembled the love of his life, his Piya. He had for a moment forgotten all about Piya but suddenly asked her, "Doctor, how is the mother?"

The doctor replied, "You are the first person that I met, who asked about his wife even before looking at the baby properly, leave alone, asking whether it is a girl child or a boy. Do not worry Mr. Ray, Piya is a fighter. She is absolutely fine now and is feeling even better after becoming a proud mother to this handsome little boy."

There was ecstasy all around. It was an overwhelming moment and everyone present there gladly forgot all that they went through in the last nine months.

Abir was too overwhelmed to speak. He simply accepted all the good wishes modestly and waited for Piya to be wheeled into her cabin so that he could be alone with her for a while.

As Piya lay on the hospital bed with the back of her hand fitted with a drip that gradually passed on nutrition to her through saline. She looked frail. But there was a glow on her face. Abir sat holding her other free hand on the bedside stool. He held on to her hand and leant to touch his forehead to it. With his eyes closed, he mumbled, "Thank you Piya. This is the best anniversary gift you could give me!"

Piya smiled, looked away from Abir and looked at the sleeping infant in the cot placed next to her bed; she faintly said, "Abir have you thought of any name for our baby?"

It was as if Abir knew what was going on in Piya's mind. The last nine months passed by in a flash in front of his eyes.

Exactly nine months back, Abir's mobile phone buzzed just as Piya was about to go out for her morning walk. Abir was fast asleep as he had had a late night session the previous night at work. Piya saw the Police

Commissioner's name flashing on his screen. Somewhat out of curiosity and somewhat to not wake Abir up from his deep sleep, she received the call in a rather anxious manner.

"Hello, is this Dr. Ray?" asked Mr. Mike Vaz as soon as Piya said "Hello."

"Yes Mr. Vaz. Actually Abir returned pretty late from work last night so I thought let me check with you if I can get him to call you back."

"Do not bother him Doctor. I rather had to speak to you."

"Speak to me? Regarding what sir?" Piya's brows cringed.

"Joy is no more." Mr. Vaz carefully uttered these words with affectation.

Piya felt weak at her knees and sat down on the edge of the bed like a lump of butter falling off the spoon. She steadied herself by holding on to one hand of a sleeping Abir. That woke him up.

He could sense something and took the phone from Piya's hand. "What is the matter Mr. Vaz?" He asked in a worried yet sleepy voice to the Police Commissioner waiting on the other side with repeated hellos.

"Joy hung himself in the prison last night. Nobody knows what instigated that. Infact his father was taken into custody yesterday and all possibilities of him getting a bail had faded. His case was yet to be presented to the court. Maybe in anticipation of something drastic he took this step."

"Has he left any note or anything?"

"Yes. A letter to his mother."

"Mother? But she passed away when he was only eight years old."

"I know that very well. But yes. He has left a letter to his mother. I will email you a copy of the same. But since you and Piya were the main witnesses against him, you might be summoned to the court pertaining to his custodial death."

"You do not worry sir. We will do everything within our reach and to the best of our ability to cooperate with you."

"Thank you Mr. Ray. I will ensure that your involvement is kept to the minimum in this regard."

"Thank you sir." Abir disconnected the call and looked back at Piya. She still looked shocked. Abir did not know whether Piya was sad because Joy was no more or because of the fact that there remained a possibility that they might be dragged into this dirty court case. He simply took her hand in his and said, "We have to remain strong now Piya. We might have to frequent the court rooms.

Mr. Vaz will help us as much as he can but still let us be strong enough to not let any untoward worry pervade through our lives. Remember we are only witnesses, not criminals."

He in the interim received an email from Mr. Vaz. He opened it to find a copy of the letter attached that Joy had written to his mother. He and Piya read through it entirely. It read as:

"My dearest Ma,

This letter is a sort of confession. I have been an inhuman. I gained my paradise and I myself lost it.

I loved you as a child with all that I had but as I grew, my brain started accepting what is not right as the only truth. I committed the crime of thinking against you ma. Will you ever be able to forgive me for that? That was my first mistake after all.

My second mistake was I loved Piya but did not live upto it. Yes ma. I loved her but I distanced myself from her. Had I been in her company, I probably would not be this bad today. I know she too would never forgive me for that.

My third mistake was that I, in my passion to outgrow baba, broke the law and scourged many innocent lives. And that is unpardonable.

I am sure wherever you are, you are not proud of me as baba is. Even I am not proud of my deeds ma. I know nobody would trust me anymore or rather nobody will give me another chance to be a person who will really live up to the meaning of his name and bring joy and peace to everyone around. I know nobody will take me as their own but I know you still will ma. And so I am coming to you. I want to die to be reborn as the same Joy that I once was in your shadow.

Your Joy"

In an instant Piya felt all her emotions come together to create a lump in her throat that choked her and she felt her breath come out of her eyes as tears. She did not know why she cried. But she did. She wept like a child and as always, had Abir's shoulder to lean on.

Once she gathered herself up, Piya said to Abir, "I have a diamond ring; I want you to sell that off and arrange for a funeral for Joy with that money."

"Why with that money Piya? We earn enough to fund his funeral."

"Because that does not belong to me. It belongs to Joy and I want it to be used for his funeral only. Abir I never keep any secret from you and it was as if I was carrying a weight on my heart all this while to keep this from you. So I thought I must tell you now."

"Look Piya, I do not care what was there in your past. All that matters to me is that you have made my present beautiful and my future hopeful. So I shall do as you say. Do not be bothered about anything. I cannot bear to see worry on your face."

Piya rested her head on Abir's chest, hid her face and thought how lucky she was to have him in her life. They thereafter did not speak much about Joy. Three days later, Abir went to a nearby temple and got a priest to perform Joy's last rights. He used the money he got from selling that diamond ring to organize this funeral followed by a feast for underprivileged children.

They carried on with their daily lives with normalcy and exactly seven days later, she found out, she had conceived.

It was a flood of celebration and happiness in both the Ray and Roy households but Abir and Piya's peace haven was adorn with tension, worry and more visits to the courtroom than to the doctor's.

So when Piya asked Abir if he had thought of any name for their child, the only name that came to Abir's mind was 'Joy'. He smiled and told to Piya, "Piya let us name him Joy".

Piya's past life flashed in front of her eyes in an instant. She asked, "Why?"

Abir looked at their son, got up from Piya's bedside stool, walked over to his cot, picked up the baby in his arms and replied cradling him, "We have undergone a lot in the last so many months Piya. Let him give us nothing but joy. Now on, our lives shall only be full of joy."

When Piya and Joy came home from the hospital, Abir informed her, "Piya, I had arranged for ten underprivileged kids to come to our home on the evening of the day Joy was born. I had already kept ten sets of toys and clothes ready. I also brought food packed for them from the nearby restaurant. I celebrated Joy with them."

Piya was surprised. "What a brilliant idea Abir!"

"Piya, it is to bring Joy back to these children's lives. And from now on, we will celebrate every birthday of Joy with underprivileged kids. Remember Joy's letter? We will give him another chance!"

Hearing this, Piya simply hugged him. A tear of happiness escaped her eye and once again, their lives were full of joy....

ACKNOWLEDGEMENTS

All creative things begin with terrible first efforts and I am only human. In spite of that I found prospective readers even before the first draft of this novel was ready. This purely is a testimony to a life where love abounds.

By merely thanking, I do not want to demean this love, adulation and inspiration that I have received from my family, extended family and friends who have given me a chance to transform from a writer to an author. Rather, I express my gratitude by promising to write better next time.

This novel is also a token of my gratitude to all those who taught me my first lessons in English.

I thank Yanessa Evans, Mary Oxley and others involved in the publishing process at Partridge Publishing for bestowing their faith on a first timer like me and for patiently taking me through the entire publishing process.

Sukanya Sengupta

I thank Arundhati Chatterjee – Hindustan Times, for investing her time in reading the manuscript and endorsing it with beautiful words.

I would especially like to mention here that while I wrote, deleted and rewrote lines, my toddler waited for me patiently and never complained. Without her patience and cooperation, it would have been a difficult task to put this through.

Printed in the United States
By Bookmasters